Lost in Vegas

Ian Jones

London | New York

Published by Clink Street Publishing 2019

Copyright © 2019

First edition.

ISBN:
978-1-912850-08-2 - paperback
978-1-912850-09-9 - ebook

For Zoe, 20 years of unending support and belief in me.

I love you xxxx

Chapter One

Ignoring the complaint from the Satnav John Smith parked the car several streets from his destination and got out. As he locked up and walked along the quiet roads he took in the area; nice houses, locked gates, quality cars parked on driveways with tidy gardens. Using the mental map he had stored in his brain he walked in a loop, eventually entering a street where the houses were even bigger, the cars were a lot more expensive and the tightly locked gates were electric. He wanted number eight, which was at the other end, he looked around, taking in the affluent surroundings and set off.

Inside number eight, Richard Cromwell was uneasy. Sitting behind the huge mahogany desk in the study that he used as his office, the tension was getting the better of him. Relaxing comfortably in this room was how he normally spent his time, but today was different. The study was a large room, tastefully furnished and decorated and spotlessly clean. It was immaculate. His desk, which was as ever totally clear other than a telephone on the right hand side, was at the far end of the room in front of a set of patio doors which opened out onto a wide terrace leading to a pristine garden. Sitting on a low sofa to his right were his two sons Charles and James, and then in a chair by the door was Bruno his 'assistant' who looked passively at nothing. Richard checked his watch; it was time. He glanced at the door and then at Charles his eldest who shrugged and pointedly shrugged his skinny shoulders. Richard leaned forward with his elbows on the desk and rubbed his face with his hands. He looked over at Bruno who had a video monitor on a table next to him. He studied it and shook his head.

Richard lowered his head, staring at the desktop.

'We have no idea who this guy is,' Charles told him, not for the first time, he had been saying the same thing repeatedly for the last few days.

'I know Charles, but the recommendation is enough,' Richard replied without looking at his son.

'From Ross? You know what I think.'

'I've known Louis Ross for many years Charles. Longer than you've been alive even. And yes, I know perfectly well who is, what he is but in this particular matter I trust him.'

Charles tutted and sat back. 'Well, where is he then? If this chap is so good. So reliable.'

Richard didn't reply. He despised himself for it, and he knew there was something in what Charles was saying, but the decision had been made. This was becoming desperate, for him anyway. He had nowhere left to turn. Louis Ross was a money launderer, and ruthless with it. There had been a time when they could have been even described as friends but Ross had become such a major player that now they only talked when necessary. Ross had no qualms about taking any action to get what he wanted, and had a long list of enemies. But despite his best efforts to keep everything private word had got out about Richard's problem and Ross had called, and offered advice, which had been accepted. He knew someone who could help. Someone who supplied services in the past. And it was a fact that Richard was becoming desperate, and he wasn't used to feeling this way.

Charles was now humming tunelessly. Richard looked at him sharply and he stopped, then sighed loudly.

'Dad, you know we found nothing on this John Smith. Nothing at all. No record of him anywhere. I mean even the name is ... ', James started speaking earnestly.

The doorbell rang.

John let go of the button and stepped back from the ridiculously shiny gloss black door. He had spotted the camera discretely positioned above him, but deliberately did not look at it. He had made his way up the street via the extensive green spaces between the houses and then emerged right at the gates which were already standing open and then he had walked coolly along the gravel drive past a Bentley and a Lamborghini and up the steps taking in the glorious surroundings. It was autumn, but despite the cool, fresh October air all he could smell was money.

The door opened and a smartly dressed young Chinese woman answered. As he began to give his name she told him he was expected and closing the door sharply behind them ushered him into a spotless wide hallway with obligatory black and white floor tiles. He followed her as she moved to a door toward the rear of the house and knocked timidly. She stood back a respectful distance. The door was opened immediately by a big bear of a man who dismissed the woman and gestured him inside in one motion.

John stopped and stood in the doorway eyeing the man who stood in front of him. Neither wore any expression. John was unable to see into the room because of the open door, so he waited, relaxed, his eyes never leaving the other man. Eventually he heard a quiet instruction from within the room and the big man smiled slightly and indicated to John to raise his arms. He did so and was searched thoroughly before being motioned inside. He heard the door close quietly behind him.

Inside the room was dominated by a large desk at the opposite end, there were discrete bookshelves with a few books on one side and a sofa on the other. The room was clean and orderly, like a showroom. On the sofa sat two men in their mid twenties, both wearing trousers and open neck shirts, behind the desk a man in his sixties sat, smartly dressed in shirt and tie. All three men watched John closely as he crossed the room to the desk.

'Mr Cromwell?' he asked.

Richard stood up smiling, and reached across to shake hands.

'Yes, thank you so much for coming Mr Smith. Please, these are my sons, Charles and James.'

The three men all shook hands.

'Please Mr Smith, take a seat,' suggested Richard, gesturing to a leather armchair on the other side of the desk. John sat down and leant back.

'Bruno can you arrange some tea and coffee please,' Richard asked quietly dropping back into his chair.

In the reflection of the glass doors behind the desk John saw the big man stand up and leave the room, returning a few seconds later and resuming his seat.

'So Mr Smith, again thank you for coming to see me. I'm not sure if or how the situation was explained to you by Louis, or if you fully understand what it is that we would like you to do.'

'No, Louis didn't tell me anything, just that I could be of service to you,' John lied. In fact, Louis Ross had quite gleefully told John in detail the problem that Richard had, crowing that nothing like this would ever happen to him, but John knew Ross all too well and wanted to get the real facts before he made any decision, it had sounded like a relatively straightforward job but in his experience this was rarely the whole story.

'I see, well I believe that is for the best. I have a problem which to be frank has completely taken over all our lives. The situation isn't particularly complicated, but I want it dealt with and I would prefer it if it could be completed the way I would prefer.'

John nodded. He knew very little about Richard Cromwell, but he came over impressively. Well spoken, he had a quiet, assured manner and was impeccably dressed, cufflinks and tie pin gleaming, his hair freshly cut.

Nobody spoke. Cromwell distractedly fiddled with his cufflinks and scratched his ear.

There was a tap on the door, and in the reflection in the glass John watched Bruno open it and take a tray and then silently cross the room, placing it carefully on the desk before retreating. James stood and laid out the cups then looked enquiringly at John.

'Coffee please,' John replied.

James efficiently dealt with everyone around the desk and sat down. Richard got up and opened the door to the garden behind him, filling the room with fresh air. He sat down again and after a glance at his sons began speaking.

'Mr Smith, I ...'

'John, please.'

'Fine, well John, firstly can I be assured of your absolute discretion? You do come highly recommended and your er ... shall we say prudence is beyond question. But this is a very sensitive matter and could easily lead to serious implications. It is important that I ... ah ... retain a certain status. I know how this must sound given the circumstances, and I apologise. It is nonsensical to a certain extent, and I really am very sorry for bringing it up, but my son ... well.'

He glanced at Charles who nodded slowly, frowning.

John waved a hand. 'Mr Cromwell, I work alone. Whatever is said to me stays with me. I don't have anyone to tell anyway, even if I wanted to.'

Richard studied John carefully. He was younger than he had expected, probably just pushing forty. And he was smaller; he had imagined someone big, well-built to be in this line of work. John Smith was just a bit taller than average, maybe six feet, and wiry with cold blue eyes and close cropped hair. But there was something about him, something hard, something better avoided, reinforced by a strong South London accent. A strong, capable man. Louis Ross had nothing but praise for him, and in all the time he had known him Ross never had a good word to say about anyone. He made his choice.

'Right, well I'm going to start at the beginning. So my first question is, do you have any idea what line of business I am in?'

'As I understand it, diamonds,' John replied, glad to finally get down to business, his interest growing.

'Diamonds yes, in fact all precious stones. I am going to sound crass now but I am a wealthy man, in fact my whole family is. My sons will take over soon, Charles is already Managing Director. But the rather unfortunate fact is we actually have two companies in reality, company one is what I am famous for, originally started by my father and the most reputable and highly regarded of its kind in the world. Company two is, well, it's not so legitimate.'

John said nothing, but could clearly feel an increase in tension. Richard was aware of the unease in the room, his two sons had not wanted this to become public and were not happy with the situation. There had been a lot of anger; Charles had argued vociferously against outside involvement right from the start. But Richard was steadfast. Action was needed.

'I have invited you here because we have a serious problem caused by company two. Very serious, and it is a problem we have discovered we do not have the skills, the basic knowledge, in fact the people, to resolve. The simple truth is we should not be sitting here right now, I should never have allowed this to happen. Now the real truth is company two exists because an unexpected opportunity came to light a few years ago and I took it. Possibly boredom, the want to do something different, I don't know but I enjoyed the thrill of it and it very quickly made a lot of money. Essentially, it is the business of company one but without any record, which suits certain parties as you can imagine and is something I am able to do reasonably simply. But I am going to be honest with you, the absolute fact is I really don't need this business or certainly the grief it has recently brought us so it is being wound up. But as much as I would like to I can't just walk away, at least, not yet. I need something personal resolved urgently, and I am hoping very much that you are the man to do it, and hopefully you will understand why I need this to be resolved as soon as possible.'

'Ok, I'm listening.'

'It all started nearly ten years ago. Look, diamonds suit a lot of various enterprises rather than money. People can have a lot of diamonds or precious stones which draw a lot less attention than sudden large influxes of cash, and are ideal forms of payment. If you are conscientious any precious stones can be very freely moved around. I was approached with a proposition which I accepted and I was paid very well. The people who I dealt with are extremely powerful and very rich. They were very happy with my work, and requested that I should perform the same function again. Which I did. And I continued to do it. So the truth is over those years I have often supplied all sorts of stones to people I later buy them back off with company one. Everyone was making money and nobody ever complained. Anyway, it grew and grew and I started doing business with a gentleman in Las Vegas, and it suited both of us very well. We essentially became good friends, and it was extremely profitable for both of us. And then two years ago his son got involved, and everything changed.'

'Changed?'

'I don't have all the details, it came out of the blue but suddenly Francesco retired and his son Pablo took over, this all happened without any warning. I have not been able to speak to Francesco since, not once. I had been working closely with him since the very beginning. Pablo contacted me to give me the news and initially it seemed that everything would continue. He assured me that all he wanted was continuation. My previous managing director Thomas was dealing with everything and it appeared to me that it was business as usual. There appeared, to me at least to be very little change. Supply and demand, which was the true nature of Company Two anyway and the demand continued as before.'

John looked at Richard and then at his sons. 'Right. And where is Thomas?'

'First part of the problem. He is in Las Vegas.'

'Ah.'

'In fact he is in Las Vegas with around a million pounds of my money.'

'Wow! What's the second part of the problem?'

'That's the part I care most about. I'm not bothered about the money. I have enough. More than enough. But Thomas has gone to Las Vegas and taken my daughter with him.'

'Against her will you mean?'

'Thomas is fifty-six. Abby will be twenty-six next year, and has the pick of any man. I admit I spoiled her, I kept her out of the family business really, she is not really suited to any serious work, and I do not mean that to sound patronising, but I would cherry pick little jobs for her to do, things that I knew she would enjoy, nothing arduous. I sent her on business trips for company one because she wanted to be a part of it, but she knew nothing about company two. Nothing at all. I kept that totally separate. She would fly to Monaco, California or Dubai and be welcomed by the beautiful people with open arms. And that was the job I gave her. We were all happy, or so I thought. Thomas must have had some kind of hold on her. It all seems ridiculous, unbelievable. As far as I knew they had little to do with each other. I don't understand it; he just disappeared and took her with him.'

'And you can't speak to her, or Thomas? What about Pablo? Can he help? What does he have to say about all this?'

'Pablo? Nothing other than to laugh and make a lot of threats. In the beginning anyway, now, I have no contact with him at all. I realised way too late that clearly he has put this together with Thomas, I can't believe I was so blind. It didn't happen overnight. I have been unable to reach Abby by phone or any means for over three weeks, and Thomas is equally invisible.'

'Where was she staying do you know?'

'I assumed she would be staying at Pablo's hotel, but I have called there several times and there is no record of her ever being there. When she visited Vegas before she stayed at The Bellagio but it's the same story there. The place if chock full of hotels and we have called every one. No sign. She is probably with Thomas somewhere I suppose, but like I said, I can't get hold of him either.'

'OK, what about credit cards? Cashpoint?'

'Her card was used a great deal initially, but I put on a stop on it. The purchases were a load of expensive household items and obviously weren't for her. She hasn't taken any cash out, for a long time in fact, and never in Las Vegas, but I stopped that card too anyway, just in case. I need her to call me, I just want to speak to her, to know that she's OK.'

'Final question, have you contacted the local police? After all, this is a missing persons case, surely.'

Cromwell sat up very straight and looked across at Charles, who found something interesting to stare at on the floor.

'Well, this was my original idea and has been suggested to me by other people more than once. But I have been requested not to do that. The feeling is this would enrage Pablo, and could actually make the situation worse.'

John scratched his head. 'Look Mr Cromwell, I hate to ask this, I'm sure you have considered it but are you sure she is still alive? Could she have been taken as security?'

'Security? John we are not that kind of operation. We offer no threat, and this is why we have asked for you to come and see us. Please understand that we perform a task on behalf of others, we are a third party, facilitators, behind the scenes. I did get some emails from her, and when she was first there one or two phone calls. All perfectly normal, although admittedly I was upset with her for going there as I had specifically asked her not to. Then I heard nothing from her for nearly a week so I started calling her. Eventually she answered, and sounded very subdued; she asked me to leave her be, she didn't want to talk. But this was quite some time ago now, nothing for a couple of weeks. And I know her John; I know her, she is my little girl. There is no way that she would not contact me willingly. And then, to rub salt in the wound, Pablo emailed me these.'

Richard opened a drawer in his desk and took out two photographs. One was of a serious-looking middle-aged man and the other a beautiful blonde woman. The man was sitting on his own holding a whisky glass in one hand and a loose clutch of dollars in the other, the woman was leaning against a roulette table and smiling. The two photos were taken in a casino somewhere. He handed the pictures over to John who studied them.

'Thomas, and Abby. Both these pictures were taken in the last two weeks.'

'Abby is very beautiful. What's she like? Is it possible she just fancied a change of scenery?'

Richard looked at his sons.

'Abby is well, Abby. She likes life. She can be a bit … excitable shall we say. Like I told you I admit to spoiling her, and yes, I suppose I have to admit I spoiled them all but she does have everything she ever wanted. She takes the luxury holidays, buys expensive clothes, has the new cars and all that.'

Cromwell sighed loudly, his eyes said it all.

'She gets what she wants. But this isn't like her. She is daddy's little girl John. It may sound trite, but it is true. She likes to travel, but she always wants to come home.'

John looked closely at the pictures. Abby was certainly a looker but Thomas was so ordinary he could have been anyone. He could feel tension in the two men on the sofa so he opted to ask a question to them, looking directly at James.

'So can you shed any light on this?'

James went to speak but Charles interrupted him.

'My father made the call to bring you in, I didn't agree with it. But you're here now, and you know more than I would have wanted you to, so you may as well know everything. My dad hired Thomas to run things. Company two as he calls it. For years everything is fine. Dad knew Thomas from the old days of the business, he always walked a fine line and Dad let him run it his way. Vegas is good for us, well it was anyway. for a while at least. Thomas spent a lot of time there, he seemed to be doing a great job, cultivating it. The commercials with precious stones suited Francesco and his partners very well. Then, as you've heard, in comes Pablo, literally out of the blue. Francesco has disappeared completely. Thomas goes over to Las Vegas to make sure there are no problems and the rest is history. Pablo starts buying more than ever, and it takes time before we realise because we have been dealing with them for so long, but we aren't seeing any of the cash which Thomas tells us he is dealing with but really hides everything very well. And now we know that meantime he's all over Abby making promises and once there are enough zeros he contacts Abby and off she goes to be with him.'

John nodded and looked at James.

'What about you?'

'Abby never said anything to me, nothing about Thomas, nothing about Vegas, nothing about any of it. And we are really close. She went there a couple of times, with her friends, holidays, whatever, just a few days here and there, she did say she enjoyed it. But never for business. Never. Dad and I are really worried about her.' He looked quickly at Charles. 'Well, we all are. This doesn't make any sense, we just want her back.'

'So she said nothing to any of you at all about leaving?'

Again, Charles looked at his father.

'No,' he confirmed.

'That's not strictly true,' Richard said slowly. 'She wanted to go back to Vegas, she had been talking about it for some time, she wanted another girl's holiday there and wanted to explore the place properly. She said she liked the idea of having an apartment there, make it a regular thing. So she said anyway. But I was already having these issues with Pablo, so I asked her not to go. We argued, but this time I wasn't backing down, giving in to her which I normally did. I didn't want her there while we were having these problems. She wasn't happy about it but didn't raise the subject again. Not to me anyway.'

He looked over at Charles, who shrugged. James looked more uncomfortable, it was obvious his distress was genuine, as was Richard's.

'Have you ever been to Vegas John?' asked Charles with a smile.

'No, never.'

'Travelled much?' James wanted to know.

'Travelled? Yes, I have travelled a lot. But never to Vegas.'

'Really? I wonder why that would be. It's the city of dreams, so they say.'

John looked directly at him.

'Yeah, so they say. I've heard a lot of stories. But no, I've never been, I've never thought about it if I'm honest, I lead a busy life.'

'So what, are you ex-military, or something?' Charles demanded challengingly.

Becoming bored of Charles John ignored the question and turned back to Richard.

'Tell me, what exactly is it you want me to do?'

'We have no idea where she is, other than we understand she is in Las Vegas. The email and photos from Pablo confirmed it, at least recently anyway. But I have to admit, we are not even totally sure about this. But in my heart, I believe she is still alive. I know it. And she is my daughter, I love her dearly. So please, find her, and bring her home.'

'Ok. And what about the money? It's a lot.'

'Yes, it is a lot, but I'm not interested in it particularly, although I don't see why Pablo should have it I suppose. So, if there is any way you can claim it then great, if not then so what. Genuinely, I don't care. Abby is all that's important. Bring her back.'

'I get it. What about Thomas?'

'He can rot there. He's dead to me. John, can you get this done?'

John stood up and stretched gently. 'I can't see any reason why not. I'll keep these photos, if that's OK with you.'

'By all means.'

'I think I know where to start, as I'm sure you do. What is Pablo's full name, do you have his address, any other details?'

'It's Pablo Escola, and no, we don't know his address, only the hotel,' Charles told him abruptly.

'I'm sure you're aware, but it's likely that this Pablo is involved, you do understand that?' John spoke gently.

Richard sighed and looked even more crestfallen.

'Yes, that is what I believe. Charles says not, but it's all I can see.'

John looked at Charles quizzically, but he looked away. Something not right there.

'I'll do what I can Richard.'

'How long do you think it will take?'

'Give me say one week, maybe ten days. Should be enough. I'll let you know when I'm leaving.'

'When can you start?'

'As soon as I have booked a flight.'

'We will sort that out,' Charles told him standing up. 'We'll get you a suite at the Bellagio.'

John shook his head. 'No, thank you for the flight, but I'll sort out somewhere to stay myself.'

'You need to go online, register for the visa.'

'It's no problem, I was in New York last month.'

Richard stood up and walked round the desk. It was not yet afternoon but outside had grown very dark, and rain started to fall heavily. Richard grabbed John's hand.

'Thank you. We have never met before but I think we are in good hands.'

Out of the corner of his eye John saw Charles roll his eyes. He let it slide.

'This is what I do, if she is alive I'll find her, however long it takes. In this instance I'm optimistic it shouldn't be too long. I will call and update you.'

'That's great, and thank you very much. Bruno?'

Bruno rose out of his chair and produced a thick envelope, which he passed to Richard who handed it over to John.

'This is seventy five percent, up front. Once Abby is back I will give you the balance, plus a bonus if you do happen to recover any of the money.'

'Good. Right, well let me know about the flight, you have my number.'

Richard nodded. As John turned to leave Charles stopped him looking at him incredulously.

'Mr Smith, I hate to be the one to spoil the party but do you understand what you're getting into?'

John looked at him carefully, ice cold eyes staring the other man down. Smug Charles was a person he could happily punch in the face.

'Yes Charles, I think so.'

'I don't think you do. Pablo Escola is a name over in Vegas, a big man. He's into everything, drugs, guns, girls, the whole lot. He fronts it with his hotel there. Look, my father has never met him but I did. I went out there in the beginning with Thomas. I've seen his operation first hand. He's got a small army out there. I'm telling you this because if you don't do this properly it will be over before it starts as soon as you set foot in the place. Thomas works for Pablo now, and he is not going to throw his arms open in welcome.'

John looked out at the rain falling. He was going to get soaked getting back to his car.

'Right Charles, I'll bear it in mind. What's his hotel called?'

'What? It's called the Acropolis. But avoiding it won't help you.'

'Who said anything about avoiding it?'

John had heard enough. He made a show of shaking Charles and James' hands and nodded to Bruno who opened the door and let him out. The Chinese lady appeared out of nowhere and led him to the front door. John looked up at the sky and walked briskly back to his car. As he expected, he got soaked.

Chapter Two

John had a flat in St Johns Wood, which he rarely used these days other than the odd night here and there. But it was convenient and held everything he would need for Vegas so he made his way back into London. He parked up in the underground car park and had lunch in an Italian restaurant just round the corner. As he was finishing the meal his phone rang. It was Charles telling him he was booked on a flight tomorrow morning. British Airways, first class. John scribbled the details onto a napkin and hung up the phone, then headed to a nearby bank and changed up a thousand into dollars.

Charles put the phone down and looked at his father and then his brother. They were sitting round the dining table having eaten lunch, which had not been as morose as previous days.

'Right well that's that. For now. He's getting on the plane. Apparently, anyway.'

Richard nodded, relief written all over him.

'Good. At last, we're doing something. Hopefully soon Abby will be home and this will all be over.'

Charles snorted.

'I don't agree with you dad. You saw him for yourself. He's nothing. They will make mincemeat out of him over there.'

'Charles, for whatever reason you have been against this from the start. Think what you like, but I don't think so.'

'I don't either,' James piped up.

Charles looked at him surprised.

'What the hell do you know about it?'

'No, you tell me Charles, what do <u>you</u> know?' Richard asked angrily.

Charles sat back grinning.

'I'm telling you. I know people. Serious people. And he's not one, he's no killer.'

'Killer? Why a killer? Why would you say that? Where on earth did that come from? And tell me Charles, what exactly does a killer look like?' asked Richard.

'Well, not like him. I mean we've paid him all that money for what? A holiday in Las Vegas, that's what. If he does run into any of Pablo's men he'll run a mile. He'll disappear with his tail between his legs and probably be back hiding out over here in a couple of days, then just give us some old tosh about how he can't find her.'

'As I said, I don't think so.'

'OK. So what do you think his story is?'

'I think he was in the SAS,' said James earnestly.

Charles snorted again.

'No way, that is crap. He is nobody. A chancer who got very lucky this time.'

'Charles, have you ever met anybody who served in the SAS?' asked Richard politely.

'Well, no but ...'

'I have. I've met several. And they aren't big men. They're not huge, muscle bound or loud, or carrying an arsenal of hidden weapons.'

'So?'

'So, they are like him. They are exactly like John Smith.'

John expertly packed a bag, picked up his laptop and left the flat. He decided to stay at a hotel near Heathrow overnight so he travelled out there nice and anonymously by tube, booking a hotel online on his phone while he was above ground. Once he arrived he checked in and went straight up to his room, looking over everything carefully as he always did on entry, but it was a box standard airport hotel room, like millions of others all over the world.

Satisfied, he sat on the bed and sent a short text message, then searched for the Acropolis on the Internet, noting its location. South of the strip, down there among a positive who's who of famous hotels.

A few minutes later his mobile rang 'No Caller ID' displayed. He smiled and answered it.

'Hello'

'Hello John'

'I need information, plus something arranged.'

'Of course. Usual fees OK?'

'No problem.'

'Fire away, what do you need?'

'I need all you can find on one Pablo Escola, plus his father Francesco. Las Vegas and area I believe.'

'Yes, we can do that. And?

'Just see if Richard, Charles or James Cromwell have a record if you can. Residents of Oxshott.'

'OK. Anything else?'

'Can you book me in to say, ten hotels around the strip in Vegas? All at the southern end. Say I'll be staying for one week from tomorrow, use my name for them and I need to be booked into the Acropolis. Make sure that reservation is in John Smith. And finally, I need a room somewhere overlooking that hotel, but use another name for that one, Jurgen will work I think.'

'Sure.'

The hotels would not be booked through the usual channels, they would just appear on their computers. Fully paid for. All John had to do was check in.

John gave the hotel he was staying in and the room number and hung up. He went to the window and looked out. None of the buildings close to the airport were particularly high, he was four floors up right at the top. Outside the rain was still falling, everywhere around looked flat and grey as if all the colour had been washed out. He sat down again and opened the laptop looking at an area map of Las Vegas. He had been truthful; Las Vegas was a place he had never been to, had never really considered, and it had a rich history, a city of legends, the scene of countless movies and stories.

But it was just a city.

John closed the laptop and lay down on the bed and shut his eyes. Sleep when you can; he was a firm believer.

Three hours later there was a tap at the door. John stood up and checked his watch. Just gone six. He opened up and was handed a package by a bellhop grinning inanely hoping for a tip, which was ignored as John shut the door on him.

He went into the bathroom and cleaned his teeth, and then returned to the bed and opened the package, which was a lot slimmer than he was expecting.

There really wasn't a lot to go through. Francesco Escola born in Cuba in 1949. Immigrated successfully into the USA in 1970 after marrying a wealthy Texan girl he met in Mexico. Occupation then listed as an entrepreneur and financier. Invested well into a hotel group and moved to Las Vegas in 1979 and lived there ever since. Has two sons, Eduardo his first born in 1971 and Pablo in 1973. Eduardo no record and now owned an electronics assembly plant in L.A. Pablo had a long string of misdemeanours, mostly minor from 1988 to 1993, felony assault and drug possession. Then it stepped up: rape, battery and attempted rape from 1994 onwards; several counts. Copies of the charge sheets were attached. Pablo had been hosting private parties at the Stratosphere hotel. The police had been called out on several occasions, and then in 1999 a girl of seventeen was found wandering along the north end of the strip, beaten and bleeding. She had been raped, and identified Pablo Escola. As the police investigated another woman came forward, and then another. Pablo was arrested, bang to rights. He was in the cells less than four hours. All statements had been retracted, all charges were dropped.

Then nothing, no charges, no arrests, everything all clear, for many years. In 2007 the Acropolis opened up. It cost a reputed $350m and was operated by a company called See Thru Inc. CEO; Pablo Escola, but Francesco was the real power behind it. Then, in early 2010, a girl was found raped and murdered in a parking lot behind some shops just off the strip. She was identified as Maria Rattalla, 21, a waitress at the Acropolis. There were photographs of Maria before and after. She was a beautiful girl. Las Vegas PD investigated but found nothing. By the end of the year the case was confined to the unsolved list. But Maria's father was a somebody; he was a well-connected senator from Colorado and he demanded answers. It took over a year but the FBI descended and very soon discovered that there were numerous other similar cases on the Las Vegas PD books, all unsolved. They went back a few years, increased the manpower, found a connection and then raided the Acropolis. They found drugs, unlicensed firearms and a lot of cash, which couldn't be accounted for, even for a casino. Pablo Escola was arrested, along with two other men. The following morning Francesco Escola turned up at the police station, and admitted owning the drugs, the guns and the money. He also told the FBI he had murdered seven women in the last four years.

Pablo Escola walked free an hour later. Francesco Escola is now on death row.

There were no other entries.

There was a list of hotels in Las Vegas, with reservations in two different names. John always carried a rudimentary disguise, plus separate ID.

Finally there was a single sheet on the Cromwell's. Nothing at all on Richard, not a hint of any illegal activity despite his admission regarding Company Two. A three month ban for speeding for James from two years ago. Charles had been arrested for cannabis possession during his university years, no details given other than a fine, and nothing since.

John looked at the photographs of Pablo Escola. There was a standard police mug shot 1999, and another from 2011, suntanned face staring dully out at the camera under a mop of greying curls. There was also a photo of him standing proudly on the steps of the Acropolis surrounded by a group of men. He put the group photo into his bag, and then opened the window, first fiddling with the lock to allow it to open normally. He put all the other sheets and the envelope into the bin and set fire to them with the bin held awkwardly outside, sheltered from the rain by the roof eaves. When everything was gone he rinsed the bin out in the bathroom and went out for a run, pounding hard around the airport in the rain. Then back in his room for another shower and downstairs for dinner.

Chapter Three

It was late afternoon as the plane touched down at McCarran Airport the following day. John had been looking out the window for the strip as they approached and then was amazed to finally see it as it rolled past the windows before they eventually came to a stop at the gate. After disembarking he changed his watch to the correct time, grabbed his bag from the carousel then made his way through anticipating the usual queues and delays at U.S. immigration, but it turned out to be not that bad. Flying in first class meant he got off the plane ahead of the crowds, and he was waved through without any issue. Vegas seemed to operate completely differently to every other US city he had ever flown into. As he headed to the exit he switched himself into work mode, shrugging off the long flight.

It was good that he did; he spotted them as he moved away from the customs desk. The doors slid open as a couple in front exited and he saw two men, one large and one small watching on the other side. Instinctively he turned his head as if waiting for someone, and then stepped away to one side so he was out of the line of sight. The doors opened again and he saw that the smaller one was holding a mobile phone and both men were checking it as people made their way out into the land side area of the airport. Of course, it could all be innocent. But then again. He made a show of packing his passport into his bag and considered his options; there weren't many. If he hung round here too long the authorities were going to take an interest but ultimately that would still end the same and he would be out front. He couldn't go back, so through the doors he went, but now he was ready.

John realised his suspicions were right as soon as he entered the arrivals hall. The small one immediately recognised him and nudged his colleague. The two men closed in on him wearing fixed smiles as he walked across the hall. He wore an expression of confusion as they neared him, both men still smiling away inanely and gesturing for him to follow them. He stopped and looked behind himself theatrically and then back at the two men while pointing to himself.

'Sorry, are you looking for me? Do I know you?'

The small man stepped in front of the big one and grasped John's free hand.

'Mr Smith, hi! Hello and welcome to Vegas. The most happening city on Earth. We are here to get you to your hotel. My friend here will take your bag for you.'

John allowed the big man to take his bag and shook the other's hand, who carried on speaking rapidly while effectively dragging John to the doors.

'So the car is right outside, is this your first time in Vegas? Man you are gonna have a great time, this is the city of dreams my friend. Everything goes here; it's one long party. You are not gonna want to go home.'

The big man barged through the doors and they followed him outside and headed left. John could see a large shiny 4x4 parked close to the wall where it shouldn't be just down from the doors. The big man walked around and threw John's bag on the back seat and then stood by the open rear door. John walked to the back of the vehicle and then stopped.

'Hey what's happening? Let's go. Jump right in,' the little man told him impatiently and grabbed his arm again, pulling him toward the open rear door

John stood firm.

'No I don't think so. I'll just get a cab. Can I get my bag back please?'

The big man stared at him in disbelief then moved closer to where John stood and reached out for him.

'Get in the fucking car dumbass. We're just gonna talk,' he growled.

John stood, poised and waiting. The big man stepped closer, his hand on John's shoulder. The small man resumed his grip on John's arm and moved in close until he was standing right next to him.

Action.

John suddenly leant into the small man with his right shoulder pushing him against the back quarter of the car and then launched a full force kick into the big man's groin, who opened his eyes wide in shock and sank to his knees. It was a great kick, way too much power, the ball would have cleared the roof completely at Twickenham, probably ended up in the town centre. In the same movement, he rotated his arm free from the small man's grip, rocked on his heels and leaning down head butted him straight on the nose, shattering the bone in an explosion of bright red blood. Stunned the small man fell back against the car and slid down to the ground. Still moving John whirled and caught the big man's hair as he toppled forward and kicked him full in the face, and then grabbed him by the jacket and charged him head first into the wall, knocking him straight out and laid him on the ground. John breathed out and then looked back past the car at the doors, where people were leaving the airport, blissfully unaware of the events on the other side of the car. The small man sat slumped against the rear wheel looking up at him shocked, his mouth moving, blood pouring from his mouth and nose. John searched him first, and took a gun, spare clip, mobile phone, a pair of soft thin gloves and a wallet. He pulled on the gloves and then did the same again to the big man; taking identical belongings from him plus an extra clip, the car keys, a thick padded envelope and a flick knife. He dropped them into the pocket in the driver's door. Then, with the small man watching, he laid out the big man's arms and stamped down repeatedly on both his hands, smashing all the bones inside and his fingers. Then with some difficulty he methodically broke each arm, and dragged him into an alcove in the wall behind a bench. Satisfied he hauled the small man to his feet and folded him into the front passenger footwell of the car, and then climbed in and started up. Leaving the big man behind he drove out the airport and headed south and east out the city into the desert.

As he cleared the city limits the small man began to come fully round. He realised something had gone seriously wrong and started to talk quickly, alternating between trying to reason and pleading, all the time snuffling and wiping blood from his face.

'What's your name?' John asked, interrupting him. He had his hand resting casually on one of the guns as he drove, in plain sight but too far away for the small man to reach.

'Jim, Jimmy. It's Jimmy,' the small man replied staring at him. 'Look man, I'm hurt real bad, I got to get me to a hospital, I am real fucked up and ...'

'OK Jimmy, just stop whining and shut the fuck up while I drive OK? I've never been here before; I've got no idea where I'm going, we don't want to have an accident do we?'

Jimmy fell silent, just quietly whimpering to himself.

John followed the route aimlessly for a few miles, and then saw a turning onto a dirt road leading into the desert and swung the car into it. He bumped down the track and then turned the car a sharp 360 circle with the big car pitching and rolling across the desert scrub until it was on the track again pointing back the way he had come and stopped sharply, switching the engine off. He picked up the gun and climbed out the car, and walked round and opened the passenger door. Jimmy looked fearfully out, John reached in and pulled him roughly out of the car and threw him onto the dusty ground.

John looked around him. It was getting properly dark now, and Las Vegas shone like a bright multi-coloured beacon in the distance. All there was for miles and miles around him was desert.

He turned back to Jimmy and sat him up against the front wheel.

'Now then Jimmy, can we have a chat?'

Jimmy looked at him and nodded rapidly. He really was a mess; his nose was still bleeding heavily and both his eyes were puffed up and closing.

'Jimmy, you help me out we can both walk away in one piece OK? I got the upper hand here, but I'm not looking to kill anyone.'

Jimmy looked at him hopefully.

'Yeah, sure, definitely, I can help. I'm a helpful guy,' he snuffled, almost unintelligibly.

'Right so let's start at the beginning. Who told you to come and meet me at the airport? Pablo?'

Jimmy shook his head.

'No, not Pablo. I mean it comes from the top yeah, but Stefan gives the orders.'

'Who's Stefan? The guy with you at the airport? The big guy?'

'No, that's Robert. You fucked him up bad man, you didn't need to do that. He ain't a bad guy, Robert. Shit I can't fucking believe this, it ain't happening. No, Stefan is Pablo's number two.'

'So what did Stefan tell you to do?'

'Look man we just do what we're told right? We don't get to make decisions.'

'Whatever. Just what was supposed to happen?'

'We just had to give you a message. You were supposed to be scared; get back on a plane. Never even leave the airport. Jesus. That was the idea anyway. We were told it was gonna be real quick and easy, take five minutes. But Robert got different ideas when we was waiting, he wanted to fucking frighten you. He wanted to take you out to the fucking desert. Out here.'

Jimmy looked around and shook his head.

'Jesus,' he moaned.

'And do what? Bury me alive? Leave me for the buzzards?'

'No way man, no way. We wasn't gonna kill you man, I swear to god. Just frighten you, Robert is good at that shit. Well, normally anyways,' Jimmy finished lamely.

'OK, so who told Pablo I was on the plane?'

'I don't know man. I'm not that high up. I'm just an errand boy you know. I don't know nothing. Nobody ever tells me shit. It sucks.'

'Where does Pablo live?'

'You do not wanna know that man. You better off just staying away, I'm serious. Pablo don't listen to anyone. Something is going down, he is fucking losing it I swear to God. Like I said, nobody ever tells me nothing but it seems to me that everything is turning to shit and fast. I worked for his dad, it was different then, he was a good man but Pablo. Man he just wants everyone to suffer.'

'I'll bear it in mind. But just to keep me happy, tell me where does he live?'

'He's got the penthouse on the top of the Acropolis. He never leaves the fucking place I'm telling you. I heard he used to have this big grand house someplace, but he sold it. When Francesco was running things we hardly ever saw him. But that's all changed now. He never really goes anywhere. He's got this strip joint called Honeys downtown. He does get down there sometimes, but it ain't often.'

'OK. What about Thomas?'

Jimmy looked at him surprised.

'That guy? Why you asking about that loser? He hasn't been around much lately. Likes the booze. I dunno where he lives.'

'Right Jimmy, you've been helpful. One more. Where's Abby?'

'Who the fuck is Abby?'

'British woman, young. Been here a few weeks, apparently with Thomas, or maybe Pablo, or so I understood it anyway.'

'Oh yeah, the blonde piece? Why?

'Because I'm looking for her. Answer the question.'

Jimmy theatrically slammed a hand down hard into the dirt stirring up a small dust cloud which drifted back against him in the breeze.

'Fucking Hell. That's what this shit is all about? I knew she was fucking bad news. Pablo running round after her with his tongue hanging out, worse than ever. Fuck.'

'Jimmy, keep it simple. I'm here looking for her. Where is she?'

'I think she lives with Thomas. Shares an apartment or some shit? Maybe. But I ain't seen him in forever. It ain't real clear what's going on with her man. I don't know. She don't never talk to me. When she first turned up she would be at the tables, and I seen her once over near Planet Hollywood, you know, the apartments. I had to go pick her up. But I don't know man. Tell the truth, I ain't seen her in a while neither.'

A phone started ringing. Both men looked back at the car. John leaned across through the open door and took out the two phones. Jimmy watched him curiously. John held up the ringing one; the word 'Acropolis' was visible on the display. It stopped abruptly and then silence, but seconds later the second phone started ringing with the same name showing. After a while it stopped. Both men looked at each other.

Jimmy appeared even more worried now.

'So what now man? You said nobody was getting killed.'

The first phone started ringing again, this time the display read 'Stefan'.

'Wow Jimmy, they're very keen to talk to you. You must be a popular guy.'

The phone stopped ringing.

On the ground there was a flat rock. John laid the phone that just rang on it and then hit repeatedly with the butt of the gun until it smashed. He put the remaining one back in the glove compartment of the car.

'I think we're done Jimmy,' he said quietly and raised the gun.

'No look man, you said …'

'I know what I said Jimmy. I'm not gonna kill you. If you're lucky. Stand up.'

Jimmy stood up shakily and leaned on the bonnet for support. As he turned to look round John struck him on the head with the gun and he dropped straight back to the ground. John smashed both hands and broke both arms, then picked him up and laid him out carefully on the back seat.

He followed the track back to the main road and stopped, pulled Jimmy out the car and dropped him on the dirt by the turning and then drove back to Vegas.

Back in the city he vaguely tried to follow the roads he believed he had taken out and eventually found signs for the airport. He navigated his way around onto the strip, and headed south, spotting a long line of the same hotels which he now had reservations in. The traffic was heavy, nose to tail but he was in no hurry. Eventually, more by luck than judgement he found the Acropolis and parked the car in the multi storey car park behind the hotel leaving the keys in the ignition. May as well add insult to injury he decided, but he parked near the top so it wouldn't be discovered for a while. The mobile had rung several more times during the journey; he left it switched on in the glove box. Then he put everything from the door pocket into his bag and followed the path into the hotel and entered from the rear, straight into a shopping area. Wherever he looked there were fake Greek ruins and statues. Not bothering to avoid any cameras he made his way through and entered the casino, where there were lines of card tables and roulette wheels and continued straight on past banks of lifts and where it was all slot machines, loads of beeping and flashing lights and a huge central bar. It was busy, the time of day when the serious players would be settling in. There were signs everywhere pointing to all the many areas and John made his way to Reception, where he waited patiently in the queue and then checked in successfully under the name John Smith. He collected his room key and left the hotel.

He spent the next two hours wandering around the strip checking in to all the hotels from his list, doing them all in order. There were queues in every one. The next seven were under the name John Smith, and then he pulled on a blonde ponytail wig and clear glasses and checked into the last two as Jurgen Schmidt, from Stuttgart. Las Vegas was busy, people and traffic everywhere. The last hotel he went to was the Mandalay Bay, which was located on the other side of the road from the Acropolis and would be his base for now. A suite had been booked for him high up in the enormous building so he made his way to his room and looked out the window. The crowded strip glowed brightly away to his left, the airport straight in front and looking to his right everywhere got emptier ending in the desert. Diagonally in front of him and far below was the Acropolis, with the lights on in what was presumably the Penthouse on the top. He checked his watch, half past eight. He'd had a busy couple of hours. He laid out all of Robert and Jimmy's belongings on the bed. The guns were new Glock 17's, both freshly oiled and fully loaded and there were also three full spare clips. So he had good firepower already, plus the knowledge that Pablo would be told he had them. He hid the guns and ammo under the mattress in the centre of the vast bed. Between the two wallets he pocketed over seven hundred dollars and a pass key for the Acropolis. That was a pleasant surprise, very useful. He turned the envelope over in his hands and then tore it open, inside was ten thousand dollars, so Pablo was very generously more than covering any personal expenses for this visit. He stashed the money and the knife in the room safe, put the gloves in his back pocket and then shoved everything else in the bin, he would dispose of it next time he went out. Pleased with how everything had started he dug high power binoculars out of his bag, ordered a room service cheeseburger and a beer and pulled a chair over to the window.

Chapter Four

Robert stood shaking in the office. He was in so much pain he thought he was going to pass out. The last thing he needed was to be standing here getting yelled at. He should be in the hospital. He had come round outside the airport and had vomited and then been unable to stand or even properly right himself; ending up lying half against the wall behind him. He had laid there for ages trying to move wondering what the hell had happened until an old lady had sat down on the bench. She heard his moaning behind her and tried to help, originally thinking he was drunk, then deciding he must have been hit by a truck. After fussing round him she eventually went for a help and a medic came out and had a look. He went back, got another man and a stretcher and after a lot of awkward and painful pulling and lifting they managed to get Robert to the first aid room, also believing he was a drunk, and then promptly forgot all about him. It was nearly two hours before they remembered. By now Robert had come round fully and was hurting badly, but couldn't move either arm properly so couldn't get out the room. They took pity on him and produced a mobile phone then made a call to Stefan holding the phone up to his ear. Half an hour later Tony had arrived with a smirk on his face and Robert had finally got out of the airport. Now with Pablo and Stefan glaring at him he wished he had stayed there.

'So tell me again, one more time,' ordered Stefan who was standing very close to him.

Robert was big, but Stefan intimidated him. He was also tall although Robert stood a couple of inches higher. He had a shaved head and smiled a lot, but they never reached his eyes, which always stared out coldly. Siberian by birth, he had a short temper and was vicious when provoked. Robert repeated the story of what had happened at the airport again, he couldn't do or say anything to make it sound any better so he kept it short.

While he talked Pablo sat back in his chair and looked up at him. He couldn't believe what he was seeing; Robert was supposedly the muscle, the one sent when intimidation was top of the list. If they needed to scare some guy who was causing problems they would send Robert. Well, that sure needed a rethink. The guy was a fucking disaster area. Black eyes, covered in blood and puke with his arms at weird angles and hands swollen up like balloons. Pablo had listened enough.

'Robert how big is this guy?' he asked, picking up a letter opener off his desk and cleaning his nails with it.

'Not too big boss,' Robert admitted.

'And how big are you?'

'Six-six, but ….'

Pablo held up a hand cutting him off. He looked at Stefan as he spoke.

'So, you work for me as a fixer, right? My man who nobody would dare to fuck with. You're the guy who frightens the living shit out of the fucker who's trying to screw me, just by fucking standing there, you don't even need to fucking speak, that is how it works am I right?'

'Yes boss, but …'

'Hear me out for Christ's sakes. I get a call. You're going to get a visitor. Well, thank you very much for the information, that's the shit I pay for. But of course I ask, is it gonna be a problem? I get told no way Pablo, not for you. You the man Pablo, nobody gonna fuck with you and get away with it. But that's another thing I got to fucking deal with altogether. But I'm warned, and that means I gotta deal with it. Same shit every day. So this guy, John fucking Smith is gonna show up in our town, and needs to be spoken to. So Stefan says to me hey no problem boss, I'll send Robert and Jimmy, that'll work. You can forget about it, they'll sort it all out. I think, yeah, that's a good decision; Jimmy never shuts the fuck up anyway and Robert is bigger than a house. If that doesn't change the guy's mind then we've got problems.'

Pablo breathed out loudly and stared at Robert, who knew he had to say something but couldn't think what. The pain was getting worse by the second.

'Boss, I don't know what happened,' he mumbled vacantly.

'I'll tell you what happened you dumb shit. We've got problems. That's what fucking happened. You let me down, the pair of you did.'

'Boss, Jimmy said …'

'And that's another thing where the fuck is Jimmy,' interrupted Stefan.

'What? I dunno. I came round and they were both gone. And the car. You gotta listen to me, he caught me out, he kicked me in the balls Stefan, I never saw nothing after. He fucked me up bad. I thought Jimmy must of ran outta there.'

'If he did he ain't answering his phone, and he ain't been around here. I've had Tony and Skinny out everywhere looking for him, so that's more fucking time wasted.'

'Stefan I swear to you. I don't know where he is. They was gone when I came round. I don't know how long I was out. I couldn't do nothing.'

Stefan turned and walked away, and leant on the wall next to Pablo, both men staring intently at Robert. There was silence for a while, apart from the murmur of the hotel outside the office door. Robert became more and more uncomfortable, not just due to his injuries.

Eventually Pablo leaned forward and rested his elbows on the desk. He attempted a smile.

'So, Robert, why don't you tell me all about the guy,' he asked, conversationally.

'I swear boss, he's just a guy. You wouldn't look at him twice.'

'Just a guy. What is he James Bond?'

Robert shook his head miserably.

'I don't know boss. He just looks, well … he looks like nobody. I mean, well, you wouldn't notice him.'

Pablo sat back again and sighed.

'Got anything else to tell me?

Robert squirmed even more, but he had no options left. He had to break more bad news.

'Yeah. Pablo, I didn't know but, he took … he's got my gun.'

'Jesus Christ! You kept that quiet.'

'He got my phone too. And Mac's money.'

Pablo angrily swept the crap he had on his desk onto the floor and stood up fuming.

'Get the fuck outta here. Get to the fucking hospital. Die. Whatever.'

Robert nodded and turned, unable to open the door. Stefan walked across briskly and pushed him from the room.

Pablo slammed his hand down on the desk and looked up at Stefan who tried to calm him down.

'I know what you're thinking but don't do it Pablo. Robert's always been loyal right? He's useful.'

'Not right now he ain't.'

'He'll get fixed up. Seriously, we need everyone we got right now. What with New York and all.'

'Forget New York.'

'I can't Pablo, the shit is in the wind, we need to be real careful.'

'Fuck that. I got worse problems, and now Mac didn't get his ten G's. Another fucking cashflow problem that I don't fucking need. Do I got to do everything myself?'

Stefan looked at Pablo. He had been with him a long time now, and had never once seen him get his hands dirty, he left everything to everyone else. And what had happened to Robert, and most likely Jimmy really concerned him, it had been way too easy. It looked like this John Smith, whoever the hell he was, had just kicked their asses like it was nothing at all, like it was a walk in the park. Pablo hadn't seemed to have appreciated that, just looking to blame Robert for what happened. Stefan had been seeing storm clouds gathering for a while now, and today's events had just made it worse.

'We need him Pablo,' he repeated, softly.

Pablo breathed deeply.

'Ok. Have it your way. It's your funeral. Get him up to Mercy.'

'Ok Pablo, back in half an hour.'

'And find John fucking Smith. He's somewhere, I want him found. Priority.'

As he walked through the door Stefan looked back at him seriously.

'Yeah Pablo, he could be anywhere. This is a big town.'

Pablo glowered back.

'So? It's our town. Find him, it can't be that hard.'

'Pablo, we are real short on numbers. I only got Skinny and Tony, and they ain't happy.'

'Like I care. Shit, offer them a bonus or something. We don't need to pay it. Fuck them.'

'We don't know nothing about this guy, who the hell he is Pablo. We need to find out. I never seen Robert take a beating, and he is in a bad way.'

Pablo played with his mobile phone and said nothing.

'It's all down to that fucker Richard Cromwell, he did this. But yeah, get someone on it. See who he is,' he mumbled eventually.

'I could call Leon?'

Pablo looked away.

'Maybe. Last resort I guess. Whatever. Get it done.'

Chapter Five

John slept well and was in the gym for seven. He did a hard workout and had a long shower, then wandered totally lost around the enormous Mandalay Bay hotel until he found a restaurant that did breakfast. He planned his day, so far his first visit to Las Vegas had been interesting but he still had absolutely no idea where Abby was. Jimmy had not been able to help much. He now knew for sure that Pablo was involved, this had been proven by the reception he received at the airport and subsequent conversation with Jimmy. At some point he would have to face Pablo but it could wait. He had watched the Acropolis for a couple of hours last night but had seen nothing of interest. He reached into his pocket and took out the pass key. Technically he was a resident of the Acropolis so had every right to be there, but wandering around behind the scenes was asking for trouble now. He still didn't know exactly who or what he was facing, or the manpower involved. Pablo could have any number of guys looking out for him. He decided to take a look around Planet Hollywood and try to find the apartments. Then it would be a good idea to get to know the lie of the land, take a proper look around, work out where everything was, he only needed to concentrate on the strip for now.

Pablo had not slept well. Frustrated and angry by the events of the day he had got his driver to take him to Honeys around midnight, but his mood worsened when he saw the place was practically empty. Nothing was going right, and Honeys was losing bucket loads of cash, money he didn't have. As usual he had the pick of the girls working but he had other things on his mind. He drank half a bottle of scotch in the office and then got taken back to the Acropolis, to get woken up by a call at seven to say Jimmy had turned up. He had been found lying at the roadside on the city limits by a drunk driver who stopped for a pee. He was in the Memorial Hospital, but nobody could see him until nine o'clock.

He went up there with Stefan, Jimmy was in the same state as Robert, but in his case he was already in plaster casts and drugged up on painkillers. He also had a pair of black eyes, and peered sorrowfully out of almost closed lids at them as they entered his room.

'I'm sorry boss,' he murmured, wanting to get it over with.

'Robert told us all about it. It sounds like bullshit to me. What's your side?' Stefan asked him.

Jimmy told them everything, embellishing the desert side of the story to appear more heroic. John Smith had no choice but to break his arms. Jimmy was busting him up.

Pablo and Stefan looked sceptically at each other. Robert stood six-six and weighed over 200 pounds, Jimmy stood five seven in heels, and weighed about seventy. As usual Jimmy was chattering away and Pablo interrupted him with a wave of his arm.

'Yeah, yeah. Just shut the fuck up, he done the same to Robert so your bullshit goes nowhere. Tell me something Jimmy, what did he take off you?'

There was no avoiding it, Jimmy told him about the gun, phone and wallet but didn't mention the pass key as nobody knew he had it. There had been a lot of fuss made recently about the odd theft here and there from guest's bedrooms and Jimmy had been as outwardly shocked as everyone, his outrage had impressed even the most cynical. Best to keep that quiet he decided, he was in enough trouble. Besides John Smith wasn't going to come to the Acropolis, was he? Fuck that. Jimmy was suddenly glad he was in hospital.

'You two really fucked up Jimmy, you know that?' Pablo told him.

Jimmy said nothing, then started gabbling again about how it wasn't his fault, he had done exactly what he was told.

Stefan silenced him with a look.

Jimmy laid there, watching, not knowing what to do or say.

Nobody spoke, then Pablo and Stefan left the room and stood outside. Neither man was happy. This John Smith was a loose cannon, and now he had two 9mm weapons on his side. And ten thousand dollars of their money. The intelligence they had received had been worthless; none of this had been anticipated. John Smith was supposed to be nothing, a nobody, just some guy who was after some quick cash. They had no proper warning and now they had absolutely no idea what to expect next.

Pablo stood shaking his head and staring around. Stefan stood next to him patiently, he knew better than to try and talk or say anything at all to make the situation appear any better so he stayed respectfully quiet.

'I tell you Stefan,' Pablo said eventually without looking at him. 'Someone is gonna pay for this shit. We should have been told this guy was gonna give us these fucking problems in the first place. You should have gone to the airport yourself, you fucking know that don't you?'

Stefan held his hands up, no point is trying to argue. Pablo would never have agreed to him leaving to do that, he was just trying to blame somebody, as usual. But stay quiet, just weather the storm.

'No question Pablo. My fault. I'll get it sorted.'

'Yeah, well.'

Still shaking his head Pablo walked away down the corridor, Stefan frowned and followed him.

In the car heading back to the Acropolis Pablo remained quiet. Stefan drove and didn't say anything either, waiting for whatever rash statement would come out next.

Pablo sat irritatingly tapping his fingers on the dashboard in front of him, then made a decision. He would get in first. Attack was the best form of defence in his eyes.

'Ok Stefan. I want this guy found and quick. He's somewhere in this city. Get whoever you need on it and start calling in some favours; find out what hotel he's at. This ends and it ends soon. I'm serious Stefan, find the motherfucker, we don't need this shit, and I want my fucking money back.'

John stood outside looking at Planet Hollywood. The hotel was essentially three buildings; the original hotel and from what he could understand two big buildings of time share apartments further behind. These stood tall and gloss black and were set apart. They had security desks at the lobbies; John went in each with the photo of Abby but drew a blank in both, and he believed it was genuine. He walked north up the strip, just following the road, gradually the hotels thinned out and got less grand. Once beyond the Stratosphere the area suddenly lost its shine altogether. He carried on heading north, past the fast food outlets, the wedding chapels and the bail bondsmen and eventually reached old Las Vegas, where he took a look around Freemont as a tourist before heading back. He chose to use the monorail from the SLS, but as he crossed the road he saw a billboard for Honeys so he decided to take a diversion to take a look for himself. It was about a half mile off the strip, at the end of a line of grey single-story boxy plain storefronts opposite a similar grey concrete apartment building and an almost identical motel alongside. In the line there was a shabby Italian restaurant, a lawyer's office, a nail bar, a laundry and Honeys. There was a big sign fixed the roof which stated 'Honey's – The best nightspot in Las Vegas! Exotic beauties inside!' From its appearance, this appeared to be misleading. He walked around the area, at each end there was an access road to a dusty square parking lot behind, which was empty apart from a couple of rusting sedans side by side in one corner. Beyond to the east there was a veterinary hospital and then some kind of small industrial park. He walked back around the front and looked at Honey's which was distinctly unimpressive from the outside and walked up to the doors, they were closed but the outer grilles were pulled back. What the hell he thought and pulled on the door which opened with a creak. Inside it was dark; the windows were all painted over. There was a greeting stand by the door but nobody there. The stage replete with shiny poles was to his left and there was a mess of tables scattered around everywhere. He could see a horseshoe bar in the middle where a fat guy with a red face was tidying up some glasses, so he wandered over and ordered a beer. The guy looked at him surprised but pulled one anyway. A girl in hot pants and way too much make up sashayed across to the bar from out the back somewhere, and sat on the stool next to where he stood looking coyly at him.

'Pablo around?' John asked, to neither one in particular.

The fat guy looked at him, but the girl answered first with a shrill laugh.

'At this time? No fucking way!'

The fat guy laid a baseball bat on the counter and looked at him, then placed a glass mostly full of froth on the counter.

'Beer's on me pal. Now drink up and fuck off,' he said mildly.

'Do you want my number?' asked the girl.

With a smile John drank up and fucked off. He had seen all he needed to; Honeys was low rent; for the working man and the lonely. Why Pablo would have this place when he had the Acropolis was anyone's guess. He headed back to the SLS and the monorail and once he had worked out how the ticket system operated headed south.

He got off at the Bally's exit and experienced the whole crazy trip through a casino to leave the monorail station. Back on the strip he headed south again on foot. He decided to take another look at the Acropolis and as he approached he saw a panel van pull in with 'AC Elevator Service – Service for Life!' written down the side. It gave him an idea so he followed the van round to the loading bay where it turned a full circle and stopped. Two men jumped out, one was a young man and the other a lot older. They opened up the rear doors of the van and began getting tools out so he made his way over.

He spun a yarn about a girl he had met who had gone off with someone at the hotel and he was trying to find her, which cut no ice but two hundred dollars of Pablo's money did the trick. They had a root around in the van and wearing a battered grubby AC Elevator T-Shirt over his own and matching baseball cap he picked up a tool bag and followed his two new friends to the security check in. A minute later and they were in the hotel. Once inside he followed the men through the building to a faulty elevator, where they pressed some buttons ineffectively and then travelled in a working one all the way up to the top of the hotel where the motors were kept. They had a key which got them access to the roof. While they went into one of the many small huts that were dotted around John did some exploring. He quickly worked out which window was his in the Mandalay Bay opposite, and then headed over to the penthouse keeping behind anything he could find as cover. There were big glass windows all the way around with clay brickwork in between, and a gently pitched roof. What he couldn't see from his hotel window because the penthouse obscured it was a garden complete with lawn and a swimming pool. Cautiously he moved round to the rear of the hotel building. There was a low wall which ran around the roof and he could see in the far corner some kind of gate, which John assumed was a fire exit. Long way down if that was ever needed in an emergency. Because of the bright sunlight it was impossible to see through the penthouse windows so John kept undercover, but he got a good idea of the layout. He re-joined the technicians as they left to go back down and asked about the penthouse. Apparently, it was only built in the last few years and accessible by a single dedicated lift which ran from behind the Reception desk, but John knew there was always the fire escape, not that he was keen to try that route anytime soon. Back in the hotel the two men got on with repairing the lift so John told them he was off to try and find his fictitious girlfriend, confident they hadn't believed that yarn in the first place but not interested in the slightest. He was pleased to discover nobody took any notice of him as he wandered around with the tool bag and his AC Elevator clothes. He went back into Reception which was as busy as ever and casually wandered over to a door at the far end of the long counter. He tried the pass key and the door lock immediately glowed green so he pushed it open. He was in a large open plan office. Everywhere there were desks with computers and people working clicking away on keyboards and on the phone. Again, they took no notice of him. He crossed the room where there was a line of small partitioned offices at the far side and reached another door. He took a couple of seconds to turn and scan the room. At the opposite corner there was another door which he guessed would exit into Reception at the other end of the counter from the door he had entered through. It was basically just a big square with no windows. He turned back and using the pass key went through the door. Now he was in a corridor with doors either side. There were labels on them; 'Accounts', 'Finance', 'General Manager' etc and he carried on. The corridor turned sharp right and then ended at a frosted glass panel door. Once again, his key worked. He was back in another corridor but there were no labels on any of the doors here, they were all plain, austere wooden doors giving nothing away. Just in front of him one suddenly opened and a lump of a man in a dark suit came out. He glanced at John and then strode past. John carried on. The corridor ended at a lift with the doors standing open. He walked in and looked at the panel. There were only two buttons; 'G', which was lit, and 'P'.

John backtracked. He decided these offices behind the glass door would most likely be Pablo's own space. Secure, private and quiet. One of the doors was slightly open so he took a chance and prodded it wider with a foot. Inside it was empty, just a small office, with only a desk and a couple of chairs. On the desk there was a printed copy of a photograph. It was John standing in immigration at McCarran Airport. So Pablo had connections, that was no surprise he reasoned. John folded the photo and stuck it into his jeans pocket. He followed the corridor to the glass door and then back out to the main room and into Reception which was a big round space with pretend ruins and a waterfall in the centre. Opposite the counters were the doors to the outside world, and to his left everything opened out straight into the casino where the slot machines began. There were cameras everywhere. With a wide smile John took off the baseball cap and T-shirt and walked around the room looking directly at all the cameras, and then went into the casino. Every member of staff he saw he showed them the photo of Abby, but if anyone recognised her they didn't admit it. Nobody wanted to talk. Worth a try. He found the two men and gave them back their tools and uniforms and then sauntered out of the hotel.

Chapter Six

Pablo slowly put the phone back in its cradle and sat there staring it. Just as things couldn't get any worse he thought to himself. Money would make all his problems go away; even John Smith would be nothing other than a pain in his ass. He shouldn't be facing all these problems; it was time to take action. He called Stefan.

Fifteen minutes later the two men were seated in the Acropolis's coffee lounge next to the high stakes casino, which was pretty much empty at six in the evening. Pablo fussed around stirring a cappuccino while Stefan sat sipping a black coffee waiting for his boss to speak.

'So, tell me Stefan any news on Mr Smith?'

'Not so far, but you know it takes a while. I got feelers out with the hotels, I'm talking to people and Tony and Skinny are hunting. We'll find him.

'So we got everyone on this?'

'Yeah. I thought it was important.'

Pablo nodded and took a drink from his cup.

'Well, I hate to say it Stefan it ain't your fault but they ain't doing too well are they?'

'Come on Pablo, it's only been a day, and they are all we got.'

'Yeah, this I know. But then Ron calls me telling me some Brit guy turns up at Honeys asking for me.'

Stefan looked up surprised.

'Honeys? Why the hell did he go there? How did he even know about it?'

'Well I don't know. But he described him. It was Smith alright.'

'What happened?'

'You know Ron. He told him to fuck off. He wasn't to know we wanted him, too bad.'

'Yeah.'

'Stefan, we got friends in this town, right?'

Stefan looked at Pablo incredulously. Friends? In this town? Pablo had run out of friends here a long time ago, his constant scheming, bad attitude and appalling business sense had put paid to that. It had been a whole lot easier when Francesco was running the show. Pablo owed money everywhere and Stefan was one of the few who knew how bad it really was. Nobody could spend money like Pablo, nobody, and nobody could borrow like he could either. But Stefan had been around a while, and just did what he always did, he agreed.

'Yeah, sure Pablo. We got lots of friends.'

'That's what I thought. Make sure they are helping us OK? I can't have Smith running around like this, making me look like some kind of asshole.'

'Sure.'

They sat in silence for a while; Stefan knew Pablo had more on his mind.

Finally, Pablo gave a long sigh and looked slowly around him, then spoke quietly.

'Stefan, we got another problem. And this is between us OK?'

'Sure.'

'So we talk a lot right. Me and you, and you know the ins and outs. You know things have been changing. We ain't doing so well, but it's nothing to worry about. I'm dealing with all the shit, you know, working hard. It's a downturn, is all it is. You mentioned New York yesterday. They just rang me. They're sending someone down here.'

'Fuck.' Stefan was genuinely concerned at the news. This was worse, way worse that some British guy running around on some bullshit revenge mission or whatever it was. New York was serious, he had attempted to get the importance of this over to Pablo on many occasions but he wouldn't listen, he never listened. And this was a big deal. New York wouldn't go away. The fact they were coming out here meant that they needed to get their house in order. Stefan wasn't surprised to hear the news, but he had sincerely hoped they would have something solid in place before it got this far.

Pablo waved a hand; feigning nonchalance.

'Stefan, let them come. Like I give a fuck right? It's only money. We'll turn things around. I'll deal with it, but just do me a favour and get this Smith thing put to bed. I need that distraction like I need another hole in my ass.'

Stefan's phone suddenly buzzed loudly, he glanced at the display and looked at Pablo and then answered.

'Yeah?'

Stefan suddenly looked up sharply and nodded at Pablo.

'Right, say the room number again.'

Stefan shut the phone off and stood up.

'That fucker. He's staying here! Room 1518. He checked in at seven yesterday.'

Pablo jumped up cursing loudly. Stefan made another call and ordered Tony and Skinny back to the hotel and to meet them on the top floor, and then called the head of security and ordered him up there too.

The five men converged in front of the elevators. This floor was all suites, which Pablo found even more irritating. They marched down to room 1518. The head of security went to knock but Pablo pushed his hand away.

'Just open the fucking door,' he growled.

They burst into the suite, but it was immediately obvious that not only was it empty but also nobody had been in it. The bed had never even been sat on, the complimentary bottle of champagne sat in a bucket of water instead of ice. Still, they searched all the rooms.

'He ain't here,' Tony said out loud, secretly relieved.

Pablo rubbed his hands over his face and told everyone to go. He stood in the middle of the lounge and looked around, willing himself to spot something. Why did it feel like they were being played for fools?

John went through the same drill as the previous night, eating room service and watching through the binoculars. He was starting to get a feel for the place. He got the idea something may have been going on, a dark 4x4 pulled up sharply right outside the doors and two men went running into the hotel about quarter past six. He stored their images mentally for later. One thing he did notice was the hotel didn't seem as busy as those around it. He knew the Mandalay Bay of course, which was packed and he had used the footbridge through the Luxor which seemed similarly full of people. Then the Excalibur, MGM Grand, in fact all the hotels at this end of the strip were all buzzing. Apart from the Acropolis. There were people there, coming and going, but not in the same volume. He wondered why that was.

After a few hours, with weary eyes he put the binoculars down and checked his watch, nearly quarter past eleven. He pondered the situation he was in. He had a job to do which was clear, but he was in danger of becoming distracted. The idea of revenge for his welcome at the airport was very attractive, but probably wouldn't ultimately lead him to the whereabouts of Abby. He realised that in all likelihood as he did get closer then he would no doubt end up under Pablo's nose anyway, so he would have to take any action necessary when the time came. So right now he had no idea where Abby was, or if she was even in Las Vegas. Or alive. He had hoped for an early breakthrough, that someone would either recognise her or Thomas but that hadn't been the case. If she was here, then where could she be? It didn't help there were hundreds, probably thousands of places she could be holed up.

He could of course just march straight over and ask Pablo, but he had the distinct impression that would be self-defeating. Pablo was hardly going to be particularly helpful, and violence could be satisfying but often not very helpful. Even with the pass key the chances of getting in there unannounced would be very unlikely, and Pablo could easily also just disappear.

For now, the only information he had at his disposal said that she was in Vegas, if that was the case then she was probably somewhere that Pablo had put her. If she was at the Acropolis there was no sign, and not everyone he had asked would know not to say anything. So maybe he had other properties in the city other than the hotel and Honeys. As he considered this he realised that this was actually highly likely, Richard Cromwell obviously believed Francesco, and presumably Pablo were wealthy. He wished he had asked Jimmy more questions. He needed more information. He considered what he knew so far, and made a decision.

There was someone he could speak to. Possibly. Maybe. A long shot, but the only one he had.

He sent a text message, and while he waited for a call back looked up getting to LA. He discovered it was less than 300 miles away, which was good as he could hire a car and avoid the airport altogether. His phone rang.

'Hello John'

'Hello'

'What can we do for you?'

'I need an address for an Eduardo Escola, home and work plus anything on his finances. Los Angeles, California.'

'No problem.'

John asked for the details to be sent via text and hung up. It would take a while. He picked up the binoculars and resumed watching the Acropolis, but decided it was pointless at the moment. He stretched and decided to go down to the bar.

The hotel was as busy as ever, but after wandering around he opted for a sports bar which was quieter than the rest with plenty of empty seats. He sat at the counter facing the casino with his mobile in front of him and ordered a beer from a pretty blonde barmaid. As he sipped his drink he carefully studied his surroundings and the people in it. It looked to him like they were mostly businessmen and women, probably attending a conference or an exhibition. Just outside of the bar in the casino a large group of Japanese tourists gathered round a roulette table laughing and cheering. Even after midnight the place was full of people moving around enjoying themselves.

His phone beeped. Casually he glanced at the display. A concise message with two addresses and phone numbers and a healthy bank balance.

That was that. Decision made. He finished his beer and headed for bed.

Pablo was sitting in the cocktail bar moodily sipping a Bellini and ignoring everybody around him when he spotted Stefan making his way over. He sat up and twisted round on his stool to face him. Straight away he knew it was more bad news.

'Go on,' he told Stefan wearily.

'Sorry Pablo, I heard back from some of the boys around.'

'Well?'

'John Smith has got rooms at Caesars, Bellagio and The Venetian. He's checked in at the lot, all within an hour of checking in here, but it don't look like he's stayed in any of them.'

'Fuck.'

'Yeah. And that's only the ones that have helped me out. My bet is there are others.'

'Right.'

Pablo picked up his drink and stared at it, holding it up to the light. Then he drank it straight down. Immediately the barman starting preparing him another.

'So Stefan, we don't know where the motherfucker is. That's where we are am I right?'

'Er … yeah. That's about the size of it. But we're still looking. You're right, this is our town. If he's here we'll find him.'

'I wish I had your confidence Stefan, I really do. We got New York here tomorrow. I can get it all sorted out but these kind of distractions I don't need. In two days we can be free and clear.'

Pablo sipped his new drink and gestured to the barman who jumped and quickly poured another cocktail, placing it in front of Stefan, who sighed, grabbed a stool and sat down.

Pablo drummed his fingers on the bar top, a sign Stefan knew well; he was worried.

'So, you call Leon?'

Stefan sighed.

'Yeah, I spoke to him.'

'And? He gonna help?'

'He's thinking about it. He's still pissed. I guess that ain't a surprise.'

'I can't do nothing about that. My money too good for him?'

Stefan didn't want to get into this conversation, things were difficult enough.

'Pablo, he don't want to work for you again. But I've asked, as a favour to me. Like I said, he's thinking about it.'

'Just do what's needed.'

'Yeah, I get it.'

Pablo looked scowling around the room.

'I'm gonna ring our so called good friend in England. Make sure he knows how much he got this wrong,' he declared grimly.

Stefan nodded and rested his chin on his hand. Silently they drank and Pablo ordered two more. It could be a long night.

Chapter Seven

John was in the gym by six and at the airport Avis rental desk at seven-thirty. By eight he was on the road in a shiny black Mustang with the roof down, rolling along the freeway headed west. After an hour or so he stopped at a diner for breakfast and called the number on his phone; introducing himself as a writer for a UK technology magazine who was in the area and hoping for a quick interview. It was surprisingly easy to get through and he found himself talking directly to Eduardo who said he was welcome to visit, he could spare some time at 3pm. John thanked him and hung up, he should easily be in LA by then. The journey was simplicity itself; all he did was follow the road signs and it was freeway after freeway only stopping to fill up with petrol and buy an LA street map. The Mustang was powerful and perfect for the journey; squat and wide, it just ate up the miles. By midday he had passed Barstow and was on the home straight. He had been to LA a couple of times over the years and worked out that he would pass into LA not too far from the factory, which was near Pasadena. He hit the city limits and the traffic slowed, but he still had plenty of time. He had the map open and followed his progress, eventually leaving the freeway and heading through suburbia north into Pasadena main. He stopped at a strip mall and had a sandwich for lunch, then made his way over to the industrial park where EEC Manufacturing Inc. was located. It was a nice place to work, groups of single and two story white buildings huddled on varying levels around a man-made lake. Although he was confident he hadn't been followed he drove around a couple of times anyway, stopping and starting and leaving altogether to then re-enter. Satisfied, he drove slowly through the park and pulled up in a visitor slot outside EEC which was an L-shaped single-storey building. Through the tinted windows John could make out people working, many in white coats.

He entered the building into a small, functional reception area and introduced himself to the young man behind the counter, who smiled and nodded then made a phone call. A couple of minutes later Eduardo Escola came through a door behind the desk and they shook hands. Eduardo was a dapper man with middle-age spread just starting and an open, cheery face. He wore a black polo shirt with an EEC badge on the front, and cream chinos. He asked the counter guy to rustle up some coffee and led the way through the building. They passed several areas of glass partition walls with production lines and rows of workbenches. It was busy, everywhere people were working. They reached his office, which was simple with a desk, a couple of chairs and a bookcase. There were photos of a smiling woman and young children dotted around. Eduardo sat down behind the desk and told John to take a seat opposite. John thanked Eduardo for seeing him, and asked basic questions about how he started.

Eduardo was happy to talk, he was justifiably proud of what he had achieved. He had done well at college and got into UCLA, leaving when he was 21 and immediately going to work in Silicon Valley for a company which made parts for HP computers. After a couple of years, he realised there was a space in the market for well-priced, complex high quality manufacturing and spoke to his father about it. Pleased and proud of his son's eye for potential Francesco backed him and they started EEC, quickly winning a contract making printed circuit boards for burglar alarms and rapidly building a good name. They started small and built the business up. Eduardo spoke fondly about his father but didn't mention his brother or Las Vegas. John nodded and scribbled down the odd word here and there in a notebook he bought in the strip mall, all the time watching Eduardo as he talked.

This was a generous, honest man, and proud. A good man.

He had given this meeting a lot of thought during the journey. There were two options for John, remain in character and somehow engineer the conversation around to Las Vegas or just come out and say why he was really there, that he was searching for somebody's missing daughter and he suspected Pablo was involved.

He went for the latter.

John changed the subject and quickly spun a tale, trying to keep it as simple as possible to avoid tripping himself up later. He was looking for Abby who had come to Vegas to work for Pablo but nobody had heard anything since. Her family were very worried. Without discussing Richard Cromwell, diamonds or in fact money he explained he was a friend of the family. He had been unable to talk to Pablo, and had found out about Eduardo so decided to try him next. He didn't know what else to do; the family were becoming desperate. John didn't like lying to Eduardo so instead just avoided giving out too many details.

Eduardo said nothing for a while, disbelief written all over him and then stood up and politely asked John to leave.

John stayed where he was, pointedly looking at the various family photographs.

'Please Eduardo, I don't know where else to go. I'm not asking you to rat anyone out. I just need to know where Abby is likely to be if she's not at the Acropolis, or Honeys. I'm sorry to come here like this. Look, I know this is not right, and it's not fair on you at all. But Abby's father, and her brothers are very worried. They have had no contact for some time now other than a photo Pablo sent, which appears to have been taken a couple of weeks ago. They have had no contact at all. I'm just trying to help, and you are my last hope. I am sorry.'

Eduardo looked out of the window for a long while. Then he opened a file cabinet and took out a folder and then looked hard at John.

'You have a car outside?'

'Yeah, I drove here from Vegas this morning.'

'OK. I'll give you five minutes. But not here in my workplace. Let's go.'

John followed him outside and they got in the Mustang. Eduardo directed him to a gas station a few streets away that had a coffee shop attached. They went inside and sat at the back, both ordering white coffees.

'So,' Eduardo motioned John to speak.

'Look all I need to know is does Pablo have any apartments, or any buildings anywhere in Vegas apart from the Acropolis or Honeys? I heard he had a big house somewhere, do you know if he still has it? I think Abby must be living somewhere and most likely Pablo sorted it out. The connection is a guy called Thomas, a Brit like me. He was an employee of the family, and they did a lot of work with your father. Pablo took over, and he got Thomas to start working for him, and it appears he took Abby to Vegas with him, although none of this is verified. I've been told that she went there on holiday and never went home.'

Eduardo listened, then took a sip of coffee.

'What I have to say to you is simple. Pablo is no good. He never has been. He has no regard for anyone, and he is poisonous and a liar and probably getting even more dangerous now things are really falling apart.'

'So can you help me?'

'I need to explain to you a couple of things. First, I came to LA in 1989, and I've lived and worked here ever since. Second me and my brother were never close; since I came out here I only really spoke to him at Thanksgiving and Christmas. Since 2011 I have never spoken to him at all.'

He opened the folder and took out two typed letters; John could see a solicitor's name in bold script across the top.

'This is our sole contact. I should explain I am a shareholder in See Thru Incorporated, my father's idea to bond his sons. I own twenty percent, as does Pablo. The remaining sixty percent is owned by my father and his partners. In 2013 this first letter arrived, it basically says that the company managing the hotel has been dissolved following my father's incarceration, and I need to re-purchase my shares valued at ten million dollars.'

John raised his eyebrows.

'Exactly. I have a good attorney, and he just laughed at it. He said not only is it bullshit it's also illegal. He wrote back and I never heard anything about this since. Then this year I got this letter, from the same company. This says that the family have a legal obligation to resolve my father's will now he is on death row. Again, my attorney says it's a load of garbage and wrote back.'

John nodded. 'Ok, so …'

'So as a shareholder I have access to the accounts. And I can tell you they are not good reading. My brother has killed it and run out of money. The hotel is hitting the dirt and he wants me to dig him out. Right now I would bet he is willing our father to die.'

'But …'

'Yeah, but. What you got to understand is my father is a very wealthy man. Very.'

'I understand that, and I have been told he is a good man.'

'Also correct, but no good to Pablo while he's breathing.'

'Eduardo, can I be completely clear about something? You may not like my suggestion.'

'Go ahead.'

'Right well I admit I have been digging. And it's perfectly clear to me that your dad has taken the rap. It's crystal clear, and now listening to you I know you know it too.'

Eduardo did a slow handclap.

'Good for you. Maximum points you win a prize.'

'Well, there must be something you can do?'

'I get to visit my father up in Ely State Penitentiary four, maybe five times a year. I have tried and tried. He blames himself for Pablo. He refuses to listen to me.'

'Why does he blame himself?'

Eduardo sat back in his chair exasperated. He raised his eyes to the heavens.

'I don't know, I really don't. Look Pablo was, well kind of strange as a kid. I mean really secretive, and always stealing things round the house. He was kind of a mama's boy, real difficult. I admit I kinda avoided him, he was such a pain in the ass. He was a bully, but he wasn't big enough, or tough enough, so he used to pay these other kids to do it for him.'

'OK.'

'I was eleven when my mom died, so Pablo was nine. She was still dressing him even then, tying his shoes for him.'

'I'm sorry to hear about your mum.'

'Yeah, well. Brain tumour. One minute there; the next; gone. Anyway, my dad never looked at another woman, he was crazy about her. Still is. But he was always real busy, and he threw himself into his work even more. Doing long hours. We had a nanny, and she was great but things were hard for us, we had everything we wanted but not our parents. So my father believes that's what caused Pablo to be, well Pablo.'

'With all respect Eduardo, I can't see it. Look what you achieved.'

'No? Well I can't either. The thing is, after a couple of years dad realised what he was doing, and he did something about it. He started being around more. He bought these dirt bikes, and we used to go racing them round the desert at the weekend. It was fucking fantastic.'

Eduardo smiled to himself at the memory.

'My dad bought this pickup, huge great thing. We used to load the bikes in and we would disappear on Saturday morning. We would spend the whole day racing around.'

'That does sound like fun, I would have loved it. So did Pablo enjoy it?'

'He stopped coming. Wasn't interested, he used to bitch about it so dad gave up. I mean dad bought him a bike the exact same as mine, but you know we weren't very good right? We were just enjoying ourselves, riding around and round and always falling off. We spent half the time eating dirt! But we had all the gear on so you laugh at each other and just get back on and off you go again, the only thing hurt was your pride. But Pablo was always moaning and claiming he was seriously injured. I realised later he was scared, but of course he would never admit that. Probably because I was having such a great time. After less than an hour he'd be sitting in the pickup on his own. So he just started staying home, but me and dad, we loved it, I used to look forward to it all week. Anyway, it kind of grew. Other kids and their dads started joining us, it became like a club. The coolest club in town. There must have been maybe fifteen, sixteen of us all flying around. Then one day Pablo says he wants to go and starts loading the bikes on the night before. My dad was real pleased, off with both his sons.

'What happened?'

'Next morning we get up, and the pickup with all the bikes and the gear and everything has been stolen. Right out our locked garage.'

'Ah.'

'Pablo must have been maybe thirteen, fourteen. And he starts waving all this cash about. Like a real fuck you. So dad kinda gave up, and Pablo just got in more and more trouble. Every year when he was a teenager the crimes got more serious. Soon as I could I was outta there.'

John nodded, genuinely sympathetic. Eduardo sighed and looked at the floor, speaking quietly.

'Well, looking back I guess I think I am just as much to blame, but there is no way it's my dad's fault.'

'Eduardo, I can't understand it if it's a money thing. I mean you say your father is wealthy, and it sounds like he indulged you.'

'Well, you were right about dad taking the rap. For him, it was making up for what he believed he had done wrong. He must have even fooled the FBI, seriously, it's unbelievable. But he knew what Pablo was like. So he froze his assets, completely locked them down. My father's money is secure; in trusts and investments. There is no cash, nothing. And my brother is trying to change that.'

'So what went wrong with the Acropolis?

'Pablo has destroyed it. I don't know. I'm serious. I have never taken an interest. I have built my business, and made my own money. It's been hard work, long hours but I made it. I've stayed well clear of the Acropolis, just kept out of it. I get the accounts every quarter, so I know they are in the crapper and I also know that Pablo is not the man to turn it around.'

'OK, well thanks for talking to me Eduardo.'

'So I can't really help you, I'm sorry.'

'Well ...'

'But, I know someone who can. George Franklin, he's my father's best friend and business partner. Has been since like 1975 or something. He is a good man, and he has the measure of Pablo. We meet up every now and then, he comes to LA on business and we have dinner, so he has filled me in on what's really been going on, all the gory details so to speak, and he is really angry. But all I care about is my wife and beautiful daughters and my father. Me and George are his only visitors.'

'Does George live in Vegas?'

'Yeah. I'll call him now, see if he'll meet you. He's probably on the golf course, we might get lucky. But if he says no, you got to respect that.'

Eduardo scrolled through the phone book on his mobile then stood up and walked outside. John watched him talking through the window, but couldn't tell how the conversation went. It was over quickly and Eduardo returned.

'Ok, he'll meet you. He says you're timing's good, but I have no idea what that means. Anyway be there tomorrow at 10 in the morning at the Hillside country club. Don't be late. You'll have an early start.'

'I'm heading back this afternoon. Thanks Eduardo.'

Eduardo sighed and turned his phone over in his hands. Then he took out a business card and scribbled some numbers on the back.

'Here's my cell, and that's George's.'

'Thanks.'

'I should be very angry John. I refuse to think about Pablo, about what he has done. I love my father very much, he is a good man I promise you that. But maybe I have been hiding away from the truth. I am not scared of Pablo, even though he has all these men working for him. I think that looking back I could have prevented all this, no that's not the right thing to say, I should have. And now too many people have been hurt. More than you know. Certainly more than I know. Find Abby.'

'I'm gonna try, but I don't even know if she's even still alive.'

'Don't give up. And call me.'

'Yes OK I will. Thanks Eduardo, I mean it.'

'Well, goodbye.'

They shook hands, Eduardo declined the offer of a lift back so John navigated his way back to the freeway and set off on the return journey to Las Vegas.

Pablo had spent the day locked in the penthouse, which was a frequent occurrence for him these days. Any callers were told he was away on urgent business, so when the contact from New York arrived he was shown up to a suite and dealt with by Stefan, who made a great display of pleading ignorance on any questions that were asked, just repeating the Pablo was not at the hotel currently. Stefan was not at all happy with the situation, so went up in the elevator to the penthouse and made it clear to Pablo that evening, who was completely disinterested.

'Look Stefan, this time tomorrow this is all behind us. Fuck this guy. We just got to keep cool, it's a game is what it is. We pay him and everyone is happy. This fuck goes home, everything goes back to normal.'

Stefan was not convinced.

'Pablo this man is not stupid, I am telling you. He knows you are avoiding him. He thinks you cannot pay. He wants to talk to you.'

'Well, he can't. I'm way too fucking busy to waste time with their bullshit.'

Stefan looked at him then cast an eye around the penthouse, Pablo hadn't bothered having a shower, there was porn on a laptop on the sofa and dirty room service plates scattered around, but said nothing.

'So Stefan, take him down to dinner. Japanese, get him drunk on Sake. Get a girl for him, put him to bed and when he wakes up tomorrow I'll be all professional and keep him busy. Tony's doing the pick up at lunchtime; get Skinny to go with him. They come straight back, we sort out the money. Then it'll be all over.'

Stefan nodded dubiously.

'OK Pablo, you are the boss. But I still think ....'

'Stefan, right now I'm doing enough thinking for both of us. I'm sick of hearing about all these goddamn problems. Just do it.'

'One more thing, we found the car.'

'What car?' Pablo asked irritably.

'Ours, the one Robert and Jimmy took to the airport. It was here, in our car park. Unlocked, with the keys in it.'

'That motherfucker. He is playing with us. You got any news on where he is?'

'No. Nothing came back apart from what we know. I got security to check the tapes. He was here yesterday, walking around the hotel.'

Stefan omitted the fact he was also seen wearing the lift engineer's uniforms, the last thing he wanted was any more grief.

'Right. Let's get New York off our backs, it ain't gonna be long. Then we find John Smith, and no more excuses.'

Chapter Eight

John hadn't known exactly how long he might have had to spend in LA so he had booked the Mustang for another couple of days. He had got back to Vegas around 10pm, and spent a couple of hours watching the Acropolis, again nothing very interesting to report. Then this morning in the gym at seven, shower and breakfast and then called Richard Cromwell to give him an update. At this stage John was still optimistic and told Richard this, but kept the other information to a minimum. One of the Cromwell's or somebody in the organisation had tipped Pablo off, he suspected he knew which one but there was always a chance he was wrong.

He felt he was getting closer after speaking to Eduardo yesterday. He knew of course that Abby could be comfortably holed up in a suite at the Acropolis ignoring her family and playing the tables every night but it didn't seem to fit somehow. He realised he was a lot more worried for her well-being now than he had been previously, there was no sign of her anywhere and nobody seemed to be able to even recognize her.

He hoped George would be a help, but shoved one of the Glock's down the back of his trousers just in case. Nothing seemed to fit together properly so far, and he thought hard about everything as he drove to the meeting. The country club was not too far in the end, just north of the main hotels and off the strip. He mentioned George Franklin's name at the security barrier and the guard waved him straight in.

He parked up and wandered around to the expansive Reception area. There was a large sign with the dress code on display; John wore what he always did; faded brown desert boots, even more faded battered jeans and a plain T-shirt. He ignored the sign and made his way over to the elegantly curved desk and asked to see George. If the lady was unhappy with his clothing she was way too professional to show it, she gave him a wide smile and he followed her to a huge lounge area which looked out over the golf course. George Franklin was seated by the window, and he spotted them approaching and stood up. The lady smiled again and left them to it.

'Mr Smith?'

'John, please'.

'Ok John. It's a pleasure to meet you I'm sure. I'm George, but you will have guessed that. Let's sit.'

They sat down opposite each other across a low glass topped table and George asked a passing waiter for two fresh orange juices.

While he did this John had a good look at the man. He was solid, with a shock of wayward white hair. John guessed him to be into his seventies, but clearly he was in shape and he had clear blue eyes that took in everything.

He smiled at John and they talked about Eduardo for a minute or two and then George looked hard at him with a half-smile on his face.

'So, you're the guy I'm guessing,' he said.

'Well I'm a guy, not necessarily the guy,' John told him smiling back.

'Good answer. OK, so you had an incident at McCarran on the way through.'

John looked at him again, measuring him up, word travelled fast.

'Yeah. Nothing to worry about.'

'Yeah, that's what I heard. I would have paid money to see Pablo's face.'

So they were on. George had mentioned the name first, and John decided to get straight to the point.

'Look George I really appreciate you meeting me. I need your help. I don't need you to actually do anything, but I am looking for a girl. This girl, her name's Abby.'

He took out the picture of Abby and George had a good look at it, then frowned.

'That's Richard Cromwell's daughter.'

John was surprised. How the hell did George know that? There was no point in denying it.

'Er ... yes that's right actually. But how did you know?'

'I've met her a couple of times. The first time in London, and again when she came out here on holiday. Nice girl, a lot of fun. I didn't know she was here.'

'Here somewhere, hopefully, and that's where I need help. Nobody has heard from her, and Richard is very worried.'

'Is Pablo the connection, is she at the Acropolis?'

'It's possible, but nobody knows her there. I've had a good look around. It just doesn't feel right; my guess is she is somewhere else. But I don't know this city, Richard asked me to come out and find her, he is getting concerned to put it mildly.'

George nodded.

'I'd say so, for sure. They're real close, anyone can see that.'

'Richard is really worried now, I was hoping to find her quickly, but I'm wondering if Pablo has got her stashed somewhere else, she could be in any of the hotels, or Pablo could have apartments or whatever somewhere.'

George smiled sadly and shook his head.

'No, he hasn't. Trust me, he's got nothing now. And nobody around Vegas is doing him any favours, if she's in a hotel then the room is being paid for. Her credit card been used?'

'Richard said it was hit hard for a while, but the stuff being bought wouldn't be for her. I don't have any details, but he put a stop on the card.'

Their orange juices arrived and George took a drink. He looked like he was weighing something up, making a decision internally.

'You in a rush to be anywhere John?'

'No, not really.'

'OK, so let me start right at the beginning. I met Francesco first in 1975. I'm a New Yorker, at the time I was involved in a project here in Las Vegas. Francesco was working on the same thing. We hit it off straight away. Let me tell you something for free, he is an amazing man. If he was here now you could put a dollar in his hand, and ten minutes later he'd be back with two. So, the project went well. Real well. My bosses were very happy, and I guess Francesco's were too, hell I love the guy. We kept in touch, and did a couple of cool things together, then the eighties and the nineties came along and then Vegas changed. Before then there weren't that many hotels around this part of Vegas, there were a few, but not like it is now. Most of the places you see round here now got built around then, place was crazy for a long time. So anyway, round about then I moved out here working on something new and I was on the phone to him straight away, he was already living here anyways. Rest is history. They call this end New Vegas; the so called purists all claim that it's lost its soul and all that bullshit, and go on about Sinatra and the Brat Pack. They forget Caesars has been here since the sixties. But this is bigger, way bigger and Francesco was there making it all happen. He was the money man, and I got what needed done.'

John saw the steel in the man. He imagined when he was younger people didn't say no to him, probably most still didn't.

'Francesco moved out here, what in 79? He had the boys already of course. They were the great American family; his wife Ann was like the perfect Texan beauty. She was amazing, they adored each other. Her family hated him mind you, but that's another story. Anyway, he was already rich but from the late eighties onwards we got busier and busier and the money just rolled in. Everyone was happy. Everybody loved Francesco. They still do.'

George shook his head, reminiscing.

'Now I didn't really get to know Pablo. Eddie was always interested in what was going on, always around. He is a good kid, I'm not surprised at all he has done what he's done. He is a sharp man, no question, and a worker. But Pablo, well. Francesco used to get worried about him and it just got worse as he got older.'

'Yeah, I heard. He had a lot of trouble as a teenager right?'

'Teenage was a walk in the park John. I'm serious. Francesco was out working and his thirty year old son was sitting on the couch all day trying to be a gangster.'

'Gangster?'

'Oh yeah. He was spending money like it was going out of style and enjoying doing it too. His father's money of course. He was trying everything. Coke, guns, girls.'

'Trying?'

'He was fucking terrible at it. He had no idea. He failed at everything. I beat the shit outta him one time. I got contacts you know? Me and Francesco had respect. We earned it. New York always looked after me and they loved him like a brother. So when Pablo hatches some bullshit plan to sell a bunch of Uzi's to some guys from Atlantic City who are trying to muscle in on some action they shouldn't be anywhere near I get the call, cos I'm way out here where all the trouble is being caused. So I make a couple of calls and it's Pablo. I can't fucking believe it. With his father's money. So I have it out with him. As usual he's got some candy-ass ex-jock getting paid to bust heads for him, cos he can't do it himself. In the end the jock goes down, and I whale on Pablo for five minutes cos it makes me feel better.'

'Can't say I blame you.'

'Did no good though. Course I can't say anything to Francesco. Pablo knows it and gives his dad some kind of bullshit and a few days later Francesco starts talking to me about the Acropolis. And you got to know that Pablo is still pulling, or trying to pull the same bullshit right now. Trying, and failing, and that's where all the money goes.'

'Ah.'

'Thing is, New York, they love Francesco. Do you understand who I'm talking about in New York John?'

'Yeah, yeah I think so. I understand.'

'Right well these guys, they got money. Real money. But they can't put it in the bank right? They can't even spend it! So they need to do something, so they come to us. Let's build a new hotel. The deal is simple. Both sides are happy, me and Francesco put our bit in but most of it is from New York. Everything is worked out; it's a loan, all the repayments everything are set. All the money gets cleaned. Francesco is happy, he sets it all up so his sons get a chunk each, but the rest is all owned by New York, and let me tell you Francesco got more than usual. But like I said, they love him, and now they got even more cash coming in, but this time, it's all legit. The Acropolis opens. They leave it to Francesco and he sets up this management company to run it with Pablo at its head.'

'Big mistake.'

'I tried to warn him, but Pablo is his son. His screw up of a son. No, he tells me, you're wrong. He's my son, he's going to do a good job. This will straighten him out. But it makes him worse of course. Now he is a big man. He owns a hotel right? He was a terrible gangster, he had no clue. Buy an AK-47 for two-fifty and sell it for a hundred. That was his business strategy. He had no idea. So of course, running a hotel is the same. Your dad is in Ely State less than a month and he starts building that fucking penthouse on the roof. Eight million that cost. Plus he is still trying to be a big man, trying to get respect. So he thinks OK I can buy it all now and that's exactly what he does, and all the cash only goes one way. He has spent a fortune in five years. Any OK hotel works in this town, and the Acropolis was doing real good at first. Francesco was really the guy running it from behind the scenes.'

'Pablo took Richard Cromwell for a million. Pounds that is.'

'Really? I didn't know that. I only met him a couple of times but Richard was Francesco's business. It doesn't surprise me. He thinks the same as he does about New York, they're way over there so no need to worry about it. You know Pablo sold the family home close to a year ago? Beautiful place it was, the little shit got less than a tenth of the value. He's got some shark of an attorney who engineered that. I tried to stop it, so now I'm banned from the Acropolis.'

'You are?'

'Yeah, I own five percent of the place and I can't put a toe in the door. But I know it's all gone badly wrong. Thing is, hotels in Vegas, they don't earn off the accommodation. It's not like any other city in the world. They don't look at occupation percentages or stuff like that. So they charge what forty bucks a room just to get you in the hotel. Their rooms are basic; they don't want you in there they want you in the casino, or at a show or even the restaurant. Look at Caesars. Look at The Mirage. Well the Acropolis hasn't had a good act on in years. Nobody goes there apart from tourists who want the cheapest room they can find or bandits who don't wanna be seen anywhere else until it gets late. And I can't do anything to change it all the while Pablo's there.'

'Eddie said you told him my timing was good, what did you mean?'

'I still talk to New York all the time. They are unhappy to say the least. Pablo hasn't made a payment in a long while and he isn't talking to them. I'm sure you understand how this works; everything is all paid for and once the doors open clean money goes back east, every single quarter that goes through the place, every month. Whatever. But these are serious people, and they get paid. And here's a big problem, there's no money. They got someone down here right now. Fella called Shawn Farley; he's a good man with the numbers. Sharp as a tack. So Pablo is in the shit, and I think it's starting to dawn on him, it's taken long enough. Till now New York is way over on the other side of the country what did he care? Now it's real. But, they won't sort it like they would normally out of respect for Francesco. In truth I don't know what's gonna happen. But understand this; I am not shitting you John. I want my friend off death row and out of Ely State. I want him back here.'

'George, what I really don't understand is where did all the money go? It sounds like you're talking about millions of dollars.'

'Like I said, Pablo tried to buy his way in, buy respect. He did nothing but spend money trying to be a big man, the main man. And if the rumours are true, and believe me I really think they are then he's spending a fortune even now paying off loans he took to buy fuck knows what and also pay off the law enforcement to cover up all the other shit he's pulled. But he's a laughing stock, and now he is deep with New York, along with some other fuckers you wouldn't want to owe a single cent to. It's incredible how he has fucked up so badly, but the numbers got bigger and bigger and he took no notice. So that brings us to now, and finally, a long time too late, he's getting the point.'

'George, I have to ask you, do you have any idea where Abby might be? I sympathise with the situation with Pablo and Francesco, I really do; he sounds like a straight guy. But I didn't come here to do battle with Pablo, the airport business was just something I had to deal with.'

'Why is she even here?'

'Nobody really knows. She said she wanted a holiday, she was interested in getting an apartment here apparently. But Richard seems to think she came over here to be with Thomas, and there's no trace of him either. Do you know him?'

John showed George the photo, he looked at it and shook his head.

'Maybe. I think I might have seen him with Richard. Maybe even Pablo. But I don't know him.'

'It's possible that she had a thing going on with Thomas. He was spending a lot of time here before he made it permanent, and as I said it's thought she had come out to see him. Richard knows she had a couple of holidays here. But the last time, she never went home and nobody has heard from her apart from an email and a phone call some time ago.'

'Look, if you ask me, she's at the hotel. But I can see the problem, it's a big place. Lots and lots of rooms. I don't know of anywhere else Pablo has apart from that shithole Honeys, but there is really nothing there. It's a shed.'

'Thing is I have shown her photo round, and nobody seems to know her.'

'That's certainly possible at the Acropolis, nobody works there for long. But, so actually you're looking for Abby and this guy Thomas right? Well that's better. If they are together it should be easier to find two people rather than one.'

'I've been in the hotel, and I've been watching it. But no sign, I can see the front clearly from where I'm watching.'

George nodded and pondered the problem.

'Actually things are on our side for a change. Fact is, Pablo won't be getting any help. He's got no friends in this town. Also he doesn't have a lot of guys left, and you took care of two more of them so they're out of action. Right, count me in. Let's find her.'

John was pleased, he liked George, and it would really help to have him onside.

'Great, thanks George, I suppose we can't storm the hotel so where do we start?'

'It's crunch time right now. Pablo has got New York on his doorstep, I can't imagine what he's telling them, but he's gonna be distracted. They want money, and he can't pay. But I got a guy on the inside, that's how I got told about the airport. Man did I laugh at that. Anyway, let me make a call.'

He fished out a mobile and ignoring the 'No Cell Phones' signs dotted around the room dialled a number. With a polite nod to John he stood up and strolled around, talking quietly. John watched him carefully, feeling the comfortable solid bulk of the Glock in his waistband. A big part of him believed George and thought him trustworthy, but they had just met and he had been wrong before. If the cavalry suddenly turned up John would be ready for a fight. He saw George becoming increasingly animated on the phone, then a wide smile spread across his face and he laughed delightedly and hung up. He then dialled another number and had a short conversation then walked quickly back; John stood up to meet him and immediately George began shepherding him out of the room talking quietly.

'Right, listen up. We just met so if you are fucking me around I've got maybe two hours left. But I don't think you are, and I just called Eddie and he thinks the same.'

Chapter Nine

They walked out of the country club and into the car park, George looked carefully around him and then steered John left.

'What's going on George?'

'This is the time John. I can't tell you where Abby is right now but everything is about to completely fall apart for Pablo. If you help me now, then I swear I will break every door down in the Acropolis to find her if I have to.'

They reached a sleek, highly polished dark blue Mercedes and George went to the driver's door.

'Get in, I'll explain on the way.'

John climbed in the car and George drove smoothly out of the country club and then headed east through the traffic, anxiously looking at the clock on the dashboard.

'OK John, here's the deal. Pablo bought a private jet a couple of years back. The fucking idiot, a private jet. Who the fuck does that, really. It's a second hand Gulfstream, my bet is he's maybe used it once. He paid eleven and a half for it. Now my guy has just told me he's sold it for three, cash deal.'

'Good business.'

'Yeah, spectacular. But now he's gone even better by getting it knocked down to two and half if he gets the money today. No surprise in saying that this was accepted.'

'Very happily I imagine.'

'He's a desperate man. All he's thinking about is getting some breathing space, he wants New York out the door. For now. I don't have the exact figures but I'm told he's behind by a huge amount. Two and a half ain't even gonna touch the sides.'

'I get it. So, what are we doing?'

'The plane is at Brook, it's a small private airfield about thirty miles out of the city. The deal is happening there, in less than an hour or so. I've just been told that Tony and Skinny already left to go pick up the money.'

'George, this means Pablo is near enough alone in the hotel! I could just go there right now and search the place.'

'Hear me out John. I got a plan and it will work out for us both, believe me. It will force Pablo out, hell he may even come to me direct he'll be that desperate. He ran out of people to help him a long time ago, and knows it. Nobody will lend him a single cent, trust me.'

'What's your plan?'

'Well that's the simple bit, we rob Tony and Skinny. No problem at all. Tony's OK, he's old school just doing his time but Skinny is a fat useless piece of shit. It'll be no trouble. Tony will know what you did to Robert; he's been around long enough to know when he's beaten, and he ain't interested in getting hurt to try and save Pablo's ass.'

John thought hard. He was already in the car, so was heading out there anyway. He could see why George was so keen to bring Pablo down, and maybe he was right. It wasn't just for Francesco, it was for his friends on the east coast too. If Pablo was desperate enough anything could happen, and he needed to find Abby.

'Alright George, I'm in. What's this place like?'

'I got a small Cessna, I keep it there myself. And yeah, I know it's a vanity; shoot me. Brook isn't really much of a place. Minimal security, a couple of big old hangers and a small traffic control tower with an office. It's normally only manned by a couple of guys. It's linked to McCarran for take-off and landing. It's handy for me; I had my pilot's license for a good few years now so I can get to New York nice and easy. We used to go together, back in the day; Francesco used to love it. I heard some time ago that Pablo bought the plane, the stupid asshole, but I never knew nothing about it. He doesn't have a license; he must use a pilot, which really costs believe me.'

'It does sound expensive.'

'Yep. It costs a chunk just to keep the plane there, even my little bird; and hiring a pilot on top is big money. But this is what Pablo does; spend, spend, spend. He's out of control with it.'

They reached the outskirts of Las Vegas and George put his foot down. The powerful car surged forward and soon they were speeding down the freeway. John glanced at the speedo; hundred and ten, hundred and twenty and climbing. George was totally relaxed and drove confidently; allowing plenty of space around the other vehicles and moving the car around with precise, economical movements. He detected John looking at the dashboard.

'Don't worry, it's all good, I've done this journey a hundred times. Look, I got to get there as soon as I can. Those boys have a head start, it will be easier to get this done at Brook than try and take any action in the city.'

John agreed wholeheartedly. If the place really was as empty as George said it should be reasonably straightforward, and he was keen on the element of surprise.

'George, listen to me. I work alone OK? I'm not trying to claim I'm any better than you or anything like that but I can do it nice and clean on my own.'

George opened his mouth to argue but John firmly and politely pushed his point home.

'Seriously George, we should keep you well out of it. If this works, then Pablo might be forced to turn to you for help but if you are seen on the plot that's out the window. I'm not looking to kill anybody. Please George, leave this with me.'

George glanced across and shrugged reluctantly, drummed his fingers on the steering wheel. At a hundred and twenty miles and hour.

'Jesus. OK, OK, but believe me I will be keeping an eye.'

The road was empty in front of them so George sped up even more. A battered, rusty sign with 'Brook Airfield 5m' flashed by. Then in front of them far in the distance a black 4x4 came into view. George spotted it and eased off the accelerator.

'That could be them.'

'OK, stay back, let's make sure.'

'We'll know soon enough if they make the turn, it's up ahead.'

'How far is the airfield off the freeway?'

'It's less than a couple of miles to the entrance. There's an access road, it only goes there. If you are serious about this then I will pull up short, we should be able to move round on foot easily but I'm gonna be watching over you.'

'I'm serious.'

'You armed?'

'Er ... yeah. Nothing personal George. No offence.'

George laughed.

'None taken. You're a professional. I knew it as soon as we started talking. I got a Desert Eagle in the glovebox, so we got the firepower.'

'George, you heard what I said right? I didn't come out here to kill anybody.'

'I understand that. But nothing wrong with a little insurance.'

They had closed up enough on the 4x4 to see there were two men in it, then as the turning approached the brake lights flashed and the vehicle moved off the freeway. George raised an eyebrow and braked hard himself, letting the car in front disappear down the narrow road and then followed from a distance moving slowly, the wheels crunching over loose stones and gravel that littered the pitted old tarmac. They travelled down the uneven road for a few minutes and a group of buildings appeared ahead on their right. George moved off the road into some bedraggled scrub and rolled to a gentle stop well short of a chain link fence.

Up ahead they could see the 4x4 stopped at a gate with the driver talking to a guard, who stepped aside and raised the barrier. The big car drove slowly forward and went out of sight behind a hangar and stopped.

'Right,' John said staring out the windscreen.

'Let's go to work,' George announced suddenly, flashing a big smile at John. 'I always wanted to say that.'

John got out the car and George followed, collecting his handgun on the way.

They moved fast, keeping behind the big building and approached the fence, which had seen better days. It was a simple task to make space underneath it and the two men crawled through into the compound. They jogged side by side to the rear of the hangar and then made their way to the edge, George fastidiously dusting himself down. John peered around the corner. There was a wide concrete apron with another huge hangar on the far side. To his right a taxiway led to the runway and there was a long line of small planes parked alongside. He couldn't see the 4x4, so they moved cautiously down to the front where John looked around again. Immediately to his left across the expanse of concrete there was a control tower with a small square building at the base. He could see through the big windows that the room at the top of the tower was empty, but there were two cars parked outside the entrance, a rusting Toyota pickup and a gleaming Bentley. Next to the building was parked a fire truck and a fuel trailer. The 4x4 had stopped right in front of the hangar they were hiding behind, with the doors open. A man John recognised as the one that had passed him in the corridor at the Acropolis was walking across the wide apron toward the office carrying a wad of paperwork, while another man who was overweight and sweating heavily in a dark blue suit was leaning with one elbow on the bonnet of the car playing with a mobile phone. George stepped out and had a look, then they ducked back around the corner.

'OK, that's Tony on his way, probably to get the money. Never seen the Roller before; presumably that's the buyer. Skinny is waiting by the car.'

'Why the hell is he called Skinny?' John wanted to know distractedly.

'Cos he's a fat fuck.'

'OK. I'll deal with Skinny and then wait for Tony to get back to the car. Whether he's got the money or not I'll deal with him, but I may have to bring him back here if doesn't behave.'

'He'll behave. What choice does he have?'

'Is this for real George? It seems way too easy. This is a lot of money we're talking about, right?'

'This is Pablo all over John. The quick fix. Tony and Skinny deliver the two and a half to him, he takes a slice to get him out the immediate shit with anyone here and sends New York away. It's a simple as that to him. The guy is a fucking moron.'

'OK, so who's over there in the office? We got no idea how many, or if they're armed.'

'Well, the security here is just that. Security. Which has only ever been one guy in all the time I've been coming out to this place, and he ain't exactly what you would say on the ball. I'm told the buyer is a guy that runs a business hiring out private jets, so go figure. Two and a half for a plane worth eleven sounds like sharp business to me, I know what you're asking and I agree. There could be some unknowns in there. But we got no way of knowing, we can't go and knock on the door. The alternative is we try and pull Tony and Skinny over on the way back.'

John looked again. Tony had reached the office, he opened the door and walked in without knocking. It was impossible to tell how many people were in the building, but everything was quiet. Skinny seemed relaxed while he waited, and had his back to them. There was a window by the door to the office but there was nothing he could do about that, and no way to see through the glass from here. Trying to get Tony and Skinny to stop driving while they were hurtling down the freeway at a hundred and twenty would be a nightmare, there could be any number of innocent people around. Fuck it. He would have to chance it.

He gestured to George to wait who nodded, and silently he crept across to where Skinny was standing with his back to him and tapped him on the shoulder. Skinny jumped and whirled around and John punched him hard in the stomach, as he keeled over John kneed him full in the face and punched him even harder on the side of the head as he tumbled back. Skinny dropped to the ground and collapsed in a heap, groaning and rolling from side to side on his back. John checked out the office, all clear so he dragged Skinny behind the car and kneeled on his chest. He searched the prostrate man quickly, finding another Glock, a cell phone and a wallet with three hundred dollars. He put everything in his pockets and had a quick look in the car through the open door but there was nothing to see, it was clear. He smacked Skinny's head hard off the ground twice, once would have been enough but he decided he didn't like the man. He looked back at George and waved him away, pointing at the perimeter. For a second it looked like George would stay put but then he grinned and with a thumbs up disappeared.

John rolled Skinny on his side then crouched behind the car and waited. He didn't have to wait long. The office door swung open and a short dark man exited followed by Tony. The short man climbed into the Bentley and with a small wave drove away. Tony watched him go then headed for the car, now carrying a small holdall. As he neared John ducked down and then moved slowly round to the back.

'Skinny? Where the fuck you gone?' he heard Tony call out impatiently, as he neared the car.

John waited until Tony was about to open the door then stood up and walked fast toward him, who initially looked confused, then alarmed, and then dropped the bag and reached inside his jacket. But it was too late; John was already on him. He grabbed Tony's arm and with a smooth rotation twisted it sharply up and outward. Tony yelped in pain and turned around trying in vain to break free but only making it worse. John left the bag on the ground and walked Tony around the corner of the hangar. Once he was out of sight he sped up and then pushing Tony along tripped him, so he toppled over clumsily with John still hanging onto his arm which he broke cleanly as the other man fell to the ground. Tony shrieked loudly and rolled onto his back staring at John in fear.

'You. Fucking Hell, not you. The British guy. Oh fuck,' he moaned.

'Yeah that's me. Sorry Tony, I need to ask you a few questions. Just answer them and I don't need to hurt you anymore OK?'

Tony nodded frantically.

'Good. Right first I got to search you. I know you're carrying. Glock 17 right?'

'Yes! How, how did you know that?'

'Lucky guess Tony. Hold your good arm all the way out so I can see it OK?'

Quickly John frisked him, recovering the Glock, a mobile phone and wallet with a small amount of cash in it. Then he ran back to the car and picked up the bag. He sat down comfortably on the ground next to Tony's head and looked at him closely.

'So Tony, I need some answers. I'd appreciate it if you'd just keep that arm where it is OK? That way we won't have any problems.'

Tony nodded.

'Do you know this girl?' John showed him the photo.

Tony looked at it and nodded.

'That's good. Where is she right now?'

Tony looked away. John wondered if he was going to lie. Maybe Abby was already dead after all. Then Tony slid his eyes back to his, and John realised he was just thinking.

'I haven't seen her in a while. She was around a lot before, Pablo used to always have her with him. But I haven't seen her in a week or two at least. I mean it.'

'Tony, do you think she's dead? Could she be in the hotel?'

'I don't know man. I never really talked to her, I kinda forgot about her you know. Pablo is always showing off some girl or another, they come and go. Maybe in the Acropolis I guess, it's a big place. She could be anywhere.'

'So what, was she working for Pablo?'

'He used to introduce her as his PA or some shit. I don't fucking know man. I don't fucking know anything, I don't even know what's going on. We been looking for you for two days, before that out every fucking day collecting money. But no one is paying.'

'I hear Pablo is in the shit and digging deeper, but I'm not interested in him. I have to find the girl.'

'I'm sorry man. I would tell you if I knew. I've had it with Pablo.'

At that moment they heard a car start and then screech off. John looked back round the corner to see the 4x4 bouncing all over the kerb at the exit and then disappear off in a cloud of dust. He returned to find Tony trying to sit up. He pushed him back down gently.

'Not long now Tony. It looks like your friend decided to leave you here.'

'That fat fucking prick I swear to god. Ask me what you want man, I'm hiding nothing.'

'You're doing good Tony. There is a chance she's with Thomas is that right? You know him?'

John showed the photo. Tony nodded.

'That guy. He wishes. But she would never bother with that guy. He's a fucking bigger waste than Pablo.'

'Right, so would he know where Abby is? Where can I find him?

'He might do I suppose. If he's sober. He works at Honeys. I don't have no idea what he does there.'

John stood up.

'OK Tony, very helpful. I'm gonna leave you here. I'll sit you up.'

John propped Tony up against the side of the hangar. There was no need to do the man any further damage, it was obvious he wouldn't be working for Pablo again. He walked back the way they entered, George was waiting at the far end. John tossed him the bag but George opened his hands so it fell to the ground.

'Oh no. That cash is yours John. I'm not touching a cent. New York can take any action they want now, if it ever turned out I had made on this my life would not be worth living. These are my friends, for life. I'm not crossing them now. All

I wanted was to make sure Pablo didn't get anything. You take it. Hell, if this means Pablo has to come out of hiding it's worth every cent.'

John looked at him quizzically, and then opened the bag. It was packed full of hundred dollar bills.

'George. According to you there's two and half million here?'

'Yep, and I don't know anything about it. That's the way I want it. I don't need the money, and my life is nice and simple and it can stay that way. We did what we came here for. I was never here. None of this shit ever happened and I didn't even know Pablo had a plane let alone he's selling the fucking thing.'

John scratched his head.

'Jesus. This is a lot of cash. Well, I suppose I can reimburse Richard.'

'Right. So you have the rest. Why not. Come on, let's go. Skinny lit outta here like he was on fire but let him go. He can break the news to Pablo.'

John emptied his pockets and threw the two guns, phones and wallets on the ground. George looked at the mobiles and then used one of the Glock butts to smash them and threw the bits into the desert. He emptied the wallets and stuffed the cash in his pockets with a big grin on his face.

'I may as well have that, just about cover the gas getting out here. Damn that Benz is thirsty when you nail it. You take the nines, I don't want them either.'

John looked at the two Glock's, he didn't need them but it meant Pablo didn't have them either.

'Well, OK. Listen, I might have a lead on Abby. Apparently Thomas is working at Honeys.'

Now it was George's turn to look confused.

'Now that does surprise me.'

'Me too. He was Richard's second in command as far as I know. The main man it sounded to me. I went to Honeys, that place is a dump. That's not a promotion.'

'Well, I'm not setting foot in there, I got my standards.' George said with a smile.

'I'm going there this evening, so drop me back at the country club so I can pick up my car, I'll run it back to the airport.'
'Sure.'

Chapter Ten

It had been a long and difficult day for Pablo. Normally nobody ever saw him until after eleven, but he had gone through an elaborate and unconvincing ploy to make it appear he was out of town. He did this by getting Stefan to take him to McCarran airport around eight after discovering that Shaun Farley was not interested in getting drunk on sake or in any of the girls that he was being offered. In actual fact, Shaun had made it clear he wanted to be up early to continue his review of the hotel accounts, and was expecting to receive the payment by lunchtime. So Pablo sat around a coffee shop at the airport for hours, until Stefan then made a big show of collecting him, who in turn magnanimously arranged a complicated and elaborate lunch where he regaled Shaun stories of his successful business trip. This was his first meeting with Shaun Farley, and Pablo was distinctly unimpressed by his short and skinny stature, thinning red hair and glasses. Pablo had met men like this before and they were easy to bully, and even easier to belittle and manipulate.

But Shaun had remained staunchly unimpressed, and insisted on a private meeting with Pablo, which despite several desperate but feeble attempts to avoid ended up with Pablo seated opposite Shaun who had piled a large stack of paperwork on the desk between them. Pablo was just glad they weren't in his own office, which so far he had kept secret. He didn't even know who's it was they were in now, but it was very neat and tidy with a 'World's best Mom' mug next to the computer.

Shaun began by recounting figures which showed a dismal performance by both the hotel itself, but even worse the casino. Pablo said nothing, just made a show of making notes. He couldn't believe he was stuck in this room, answering bullshit questions from some half Irish midget that a bunch of faceless nobodies in New York had sent to see him.

There were sheets of numbers and then an annual spreadsheet containing a graph with a distinctly downward facing red line, and then monthly breakdowns with even more numbers in red, which were all explained in detail to Pablo who tuned it out; wondering when it would all be over.

Eventually Shaun laid down his Montblanc pen and pushed his glasses up his nose. He stared at Pablo who began to sweat.

'You do appreciate Pablo, the leniency that my employers have shown you out of the deep respect for your father.'

'My father!' spat Pablo.

Shaun made no effort to be placatory.

'If your father were here, I doubt very much I would need to be.'

'Yeah, yeah. My father the saint. Look Shaun, you don't need to worry.'

'I'm not worried.'

'Well, whatever but you are getting your money today. It's not my fault; the whole world has bad debts right?'

'There are no significant debtors on your accounts Pablo. Plenty of creditors.'

'What? Well, yes but you have to understand I'm a businessman, I have many other concerns.'

'What concerns Pablo? Honeys is making a loss in excess of a quarter of a million per year to date. I see no other lines of income.'

'I have many business interests. Like I said, I'm a businessman. Like my father.'

'You are nothing like your father.'

Pablo stood up outraged.

'Well if you flew out here just to insult me then …'

'Then what Pablo?'

Shaun sat, perfectly relaxed, unnerving Pablo even more.

'As I said, you'll get your money. By 2pm today. Then you can get on a plane.'

'Right. So, just how much will you be paying us today?'

'Two million dollars,' Pablo announced triumphantly.

'Hmmm.'

Shaun slowly leafed through some paperwork, and then removed yet another detailed sheet and glanced at it, then turned it around and carefully placed it in front of Pablo, who also looked at it but it made no sense to him; it was just numbers. Lots of red ink.

'Yeah, so what?'

'That shows you currently owe us over twenty-one million Pablo. Twenty-one million dollars.'

The paperwork swam in front of Pablo's eyes and he gripped the edge of the desk. Twenty-one million? How the fuck did that happen? This had to be bullshit, those motherfuckers in New York were treating him like he was some kind of asshole. But he knew that there had been no payments for a while, and that there was a strict agreement. There always had been. Reluctantly he had to admit to himself that the finance guys had been on at him, and he had been ignoring phone calls for longer than he could remember. He recovered, all he had to do was put on a front. Two million and then Shaun would leave him in peace. He would work out the rest.

'Yeah, yeah, of course, I am aware of that. Business is tough right now. I'm doing what I can with my hotel. What can I do?'

'Your hotel? Pablo, you do understand our relationship, right? We own this building. You don't. It is ours, we bought the land, and we built it, all paid for. You have entered into a contract with us to run the hotel, that is what your company does, you are the CEO. In return, you take a share of the profits, the numbers are previously agreed in the contract, all the percentages, expenses, repairs, dilapidations, everything. In turn, we pay out to our shareholders, one of which is of course your own father. Now how can we be expected to make our payments, when you are not making yours.'

His father. Getting paid all the time he was in prison.

'Yeah, about that, my father thought his share should come to me for the time being, you know, as I turn this baby around.'

Shaun flicked through more paperwork.

'No, the instruction is to pay into a fund, which was established, what, three years ago. No changes have been requested, and I am certainly not about to take your word on anything. Now, getting back to the reality of the situation, what do you propose to do about the fact you own us twenty-one million dollars?'

'Well, yeah, but this is business and I was thinking that I could pay two million now, and ...'

'Pay us another two million next month, and so on? On top of the scheduled payments, which you have been missing.'

'Maybe not in a month, but soon. You know. Like I said, business is bad, but I'll turn it around.'

'How will you do that? Pablo, let's just go back to basics. I'm not sure you completely understand the situation, which is actually perfectly clear. Let's assume, that I want to drive a cab, right here in Las Vegas, but I don't have a car. So, let's say you loan me a thousand bucks, for a year. I get the cash, and buy a car. But then I find out I'm one cab in hundreds of others, and I'm not making the money. Now, where does that leave you?'

'What?'

'What happens to your loan? Does it get repaid?'

Pablo was sweating even more now, but then he realised that Farley had let him off the hook, the dumb asshole.

'Well, I would extend it. I'd help out.'

'Would you? So I don't make my monthly repayment. You wouldn't request your eighty-three dollars and thirty-three cents, you would let me off it completely.'

'Well, no, but I would accept less, I would be helpful, give you time to pay me back.'

That should shut the ginger midget up. At last.

But Farley stared back at him.

'OK, I see, I understand it now. Right, yeah, I see that you would be reasonable. Like maybe say, somebody giving someone else time to make payments, for example, despite not hearing a damn word. And let's just say you discovered that actually I did have it, but frittered it away on endless crap, buying and selling and losing every time, just to try to impress people, which effectively, you are funding. What would you say to me then?'

Fuck. He'd walked right into that. Why didn't he keep his goddamned mouth shut?

'Er, well I ....'

But Farley, clearly bored by now, cut him off.

'I could ring New York now, but we both know what they will say. Two million is not enough.'

'OK, two and half.'

Pablo cursed inwardly as he spoke, hating it that he had no other choice. He desperately needed the half million just to keep his few remaining people onside.

Shaun stood up.

'I'll make the call. Stay here. You're going to have to tell me exactly how you will raise the remaining eighteen and a half million, plus interest, and when we should expect it.'

He left the room. Pablo stood up, indignant at being treated like a child, but realised there was nowhere he could go. Irritated he paced the room checking the time. It was gone eleven, in a couple of hours this crap would be behind him.

Shaun returned all too quickly and closed the door quietly behind him. He sat down and waited for Pablo to do the same.

'Two point five today. Then the same within sixty days, and then a repeat. And you make the payments on time. The current debt is to be paid within the next thirty-six months, along with all the normal amounts. No payments can be missed, and that has to be understood. And there will be interest, this has become a loan. I don't believe I need to explain to you that this is the last chance you will get. We've been trying to discuss this problem with you for months.'

Pablo looked at his watch; time seemed to have frozen still.

'Fine,' he replied dully. 'That's fine.'

'Pablo, if you do manage to make this payment today, which I have to say I doubt, then how will you raise two and half million dollars in sixty days?'

'That's my problem.'

Shaun stood up and leaned over the desk. Pablo warily moved back, hating himself for doing it. He could break this skinny Irish motherfucker into pieces, and he was very close to doing it. Not him personally of course, but Stefan would soon get it done. If only he could get the hell out of this office.

Shaun spoke patiently, as if addressing a wilful child.

'No, it's mine Pablo. It means I will be back, and I won't be alone. I am truly sorry for your father, he hasn't done anything wrong other than try his best for you. But next time things will be very different. I have some more work to do, I will be waiting.'

Shaun left the room and Pablo sat for a while, as the situation he was in sunk in.

Now, he stood on the balcony up in the champagne bar on the fifteenth floor looking out over South Las Vegas Boulevard. He watched a Ferrari accelerate away from the lights further down and wished he was driving it. He had owned a Ferrari once, but that was gone; sold like everything else. More cash that had disappeared. He sighed and looked back into the bar, seeing the empty chairs and tables and the tired façade properly for the first time. He remembered when the Acropolis first opened, this balcony was full of the beautiful people, and they would take bookings for seats outside right where he was standing. Now, at lunchtime, he was the only patron. He rested his head on the glass and peered over the balcony wall at the roof of the Acropolis Dome below. He couldn't remember the last time there had been a show on; he had last been in the Dome at Christmas a few years ago. For the millionth time that day he checked his watch. Tony and Skinny would be there by now. This would soon all be over.

Stefan didn't like Honeys, and went out of his way to avoid going there. But right now, he was just happy to get away from the Acropolis, Pablo was driving him crazy with how he was dealing with everything, or not dealing with anything at all, and the New York situation was only going to worse.

He sat at a table to one side on his own, nursing an orange juice. There were only another five or six customers there, a couple of them watching a moody looking girl with long black hair wander around the stage in bright green hot pants, the rest sitting round the bar chatting to Ron. He'd been surprised when Stefan had walked in, and immediately wary. But Stefan had done nothing more than ask him for an orange juice and then gone and sat down.

Fifteen minutes later Leon Vries walked in, and dropped into a seat opposite.

Ron appeared immediately, Leon asked for a beer.

'Sorry I'm late Stefan, fucking traffic is even more shit than usual.'

Stefan was annoyed, but said nothing. Instead, he pulled out the photo of John Smith.

'I need you to find out all about this guy Leon. His name's John Smith, he's from London.'

Leon looked at the picture.

'He causing you trouble? Doesn't look the type.'

'Yeah, well, I got to know.'

'He ain't the guy? The one that fucked up Robert? It can't be him?'

Stefan pursed his lips.

'Yeah, it's this guy. Look Leon, I just need this doing OK? We don't know nothing about him, all we got so far is bullshit it seems.'

Leon sat back while Ron placed a bottle in front of him, and then took a drink.

'If you ask me, Pablo had this shit coming a long ways. But just if you ask me.'

'I ain't arguing with you Leon. But this is for me.'

'Pablo don't know you're here?'

'No.'

Leon raised his eyebrows.

'Well, OK. Cos I ain't doing nothing for that motherfucker Pablo, and I told you that already. If he gets himself fucked up then I'm real happy about it. He owes me money, and that's just for starters. And you know all about that Stefan.'

Stefan sighed.

'He owes everybody money Leon.'

'Yeah I heard that, and he needs to learn respect. But OK, as it's you I'll see what I can find. But this is just for you, understand?'

Stefan stood up and shook the other man's hand.

'Thanks Leon, I better get back to the hotel.'

He walked out of Honeys leaving Leon to start tapping into his mobile. Hopefully he would find something out and soon.

Chapter Eleven

An hour later back at the Acropolis and Stefan got the call. Leon had found out exactly who John Smith was, and it was not good news, not good at all. Stefan was getting more irritated by the second. No sign of Tony or Skinny and no answer from either of them on their phones so once again Pablo had asked him to distract Shaun, which just as before was impossible. Shaun sat perfectly still in the VIP lounge with a glass of water and waited, completely disinterested in Stefan who gave up and stood at the entrance looking out. This was getting tedious he thought. As he stared moodily across the casino he suddenly caught sight of Skinny slouching across Reception and without saying anything to Shaun set off after him.

Skinny made his way straight to Pablo's office and Stefan followed him in through the door. Pablo looked up as they entered but his beaming smile dropped when he saw the livid marks on the side of Skinny's face and the dishevelled clothing.

And nothing in the man's hands.

'It's gone boss. Taken. It was Smith. He came out of nowhere.' Skinny looked like he was about to cry.

Pablo just sat there frozen, staring at nothing, his mouth opening and closing like a goldfish.

Stefan ignored Skinny completely.

'Boss. This John Smith. I found shit out about him. He was special forces. This is not a guy you fuck with.'

Pablo shook his head.

'No, bullshit. Nobody fucks with me. Not in my hotel, in my town.'

'Pablo …'

'What! What do you want for Christ's sakes, I'm thinking here.'

'You need to speak to Shaun, and right now. This can't carry on. New York need to know the truth.'

Pablo looked up at him feverishly but said nothing. He began drumming his fingers on the desk, then stood up and sat straight back down again.

Stefan watched him impatiently.

'Pablo …'

'No, what I need is to get Shaun fucking Farley out the way. Take care of it Stefan; make sure he's never found. It'll buy us time until we get hold of Smith, then everything will take care of itself,' Pablo spoke fast and breathlessly.

Stefan stared at Pablo incredulously.

'Pablo, just wait … what! … are you telling me to kill Shaun Farley?'

'Of course! Don't you see, it's the simple solution. Just get rid of him, and quick. Just do it. Then you and Skinny drop him somewhere in the desert. Make sure the little Irish shit is never found. Who cares.'

'Pablo, I don't think that you understand what you're saying. You need …'

Pablo interrupted him raising his voice.

'No Stefan! You don't tell me what I need! I tell you! You listen to me! Listen to me! I'm in charge! You do what I say! I am telling you to kill him. Do it, go!'

Stefan stared at him, and then smiled. He stepped forward, pushing Skinny to one side. He reached in his jacket and took out his Glock and mobile phone. Calmly, he laid them out on the desk. Pablo looked down at them as if he had never seen them before.

'That's it Pablo. You can have these back. I'm out. It's all gone to shit. You are seriously asking me to kill someone, and not just anyone. Shaun is New York. Fuck that. This job ain't doing any of us any good, and I don't want it anymore.'

Skinny saw his chance and jumped in immediately, this was a distraction from him losing the money and Stefan always gave him a hard time.

'Good riddance Pablo, we don't need him. First out the door when things get tough right?'

Stefan grabbed Skinny by the lapels and pushed him against the wall.

'Job's yours Skinny you prick. All yours.'

He kicked out Skinny's ankles from underneath and the fat man fell to the floor with a loud thump. Stefan reached down and grabbed hold of his hair, then leaned in close to his face.

'Tell you what tough guy. Make it that the first thing that you do is throw me out. Do it.'

Skinny wouldn't meet his eye.

Stefan thumped his head back against the wall and let go, then pulled open the office door and left without looking back.

Pablo sat very still watching and then suddenly snapped and jumped out running after him into the corridor.

'You fuck off Stefan! Fuck off! You're nothing! I made you, where you gonna go? Fuck off then,' he shrieked, shaking and eyes wild with fury.

Stefan ignored it. He had known for longer than he cared to admit that it had only been a matter of time. He had been hanging on out of a crazy sense of loyalty to Francesco, who had requested something of him, something which was now too much. He knew that he was just one of many others who had been asked to look out for Pablo by his father. But not any longer, enough was enough. John Smith and Shaun Farley had been a long time coming, Pablo had been getting away with it forever. The debts were piling up, and he either ignored or dismissed them. It was time to go. He walked out into Reception and made his way through the casino to the VIP bar. Shaun Farley was seated in the same place, and watched Stefan calmly as he threaded his way over.

'I'm sorry Shaun. This is all bullshit, but I suspect you already know. There's no money. It's over,' Stefan told him simply and then left.

He crossed back through the casino and used his pass key to walk into the cashier's office. The staff there looked at him curiously as he opened the safe and took out twenty thousand dollars. He hadn't been paid properly in three months, and the balance he would give to Robert and Jimmy. He shoved the cash into his inside jacket pocket, threw his pass key on the floor and walked out of the office and then left the hotel.

Outside he walked to the bottom of the steps and stopped. He turned around and looked up and stretched his arms out wide smiling. The world had been lifted from his shoulders.

'Goodbye.'

Pablo walked back into the office and slammed the door. He sat down hard at the desk breathing deeply. That fucking Stefan. No loyalty. Well he would show him, he would come crawling back. This was just a temporary setback. But right now he needed help. Only one thing to do, and maybe he should have done it in the first place.

Skinny puffed himself up and told Pablo he would take care of Shaun, but Pablo came to his senses. That would just be a disaster. Skinny would fuck it up and there would be even more heat he didn't need.

He told Skinny to go and find Shaun Farley and apologise for the delay. Just make up any old bullshit, and then come straight back. Once he was alone he picked up his mobile and went through the phone book.

Chapter Twelve

Frank MacMillan walked into the precinct building and crossed the squad room, helping himself to a couple of doughnuts on the way. He glanced at his watch, it had gone three already. Excellent. By five he could be out the door. Have a couple at Circus Circus on his way home. As he sat down behind his desk happily wondering how he could waste the next couple of hours his private mobile began to vibrate in his pocket.

Frank MacMillan was a lieutenant in the Las Vegas police department. He was fifty-four years old, overweight, lazy, and corrupt.

He could have retired six years ago after twenty-five years in but the benefits were just too good. Turning a blind eye, hiding various incriminating details, losing evidence, tipping off certain individuals. Everything worked out very well for MacMillan, he had been cultivating it for years. He was protected of course, by the badge he wore but more by the very people that he was supposed be keeping on the straight and narrow. He had moved out to Vegas in 1992 as a detective from Seattle, where he was already making a few dollars extra here and there. He calculated, rightly, that there would be even more opportunities further South and had ended up staying, winning promotions by making sure he was right at the forefront with his name involved somewhere of any actual arrests and ensuring he was always in the right place at the right time. The new Las Vegas South Precinct had opened in 2011 and MacMillan had immediately put himself forward. The precinct was a lot quieter than the day to day machinations of the Metropolitan Precinct, so MacMillan was able to take it even easier. The overall crime rate in Las Vegas had been dropping for two years, but there was a growing gang problem in the city that he was glad to get away from, there was nothing to be earned from those guys. Visitors to Vegas only really saw the strip, but there was a maze of suburbs behind the scenes, with bars, strip joints, night clubs all presenting not only a constant source of crime, but a substantial source of additional revenue if you knew where to look and who to nudge. South Precinct was built in expectation of growth, the houses and apartments were more expensive here; the streets around were quiet and the PD there only dealt with that end of the strip. There were only thirty full time officers at the precinct; he had a team of three detectives under him, all young guys. He kept them well away from anyone that mattered and let them deal with the domestic problems, car crimes, street robberies etc. All in all, MacMillan had it all sown up.

But over the last eighteen months or so things had been changing, and fast. The old guard were out. Back in the day MacMillan could rely on getting his ass covered, but not any longer. The DA had ended up in prison. MacMillan's own chief had joined him. There was an investigation going on right now into corruption, and there were a lot of very worried senior policemen all over the city that were feeling the heat. MacMillan realized all too well that his name would keep cropping up, although the investigation had bigger fish to fry at this stage and had decided a while ago to call it a day, but had opted to not hand his resignation in immediately to avoid any additional suspicion. But things were getting more and more difficult, the lawyers were demanding blood. There were changes everywhere, he had a new captain now, who had not so tactfully suggested that MacMillan may want to look outside the police force as a career. He had six months at most, and was determined to rake in every cent possible.

It was MacMillan that dealt with Pablo back in the early days. Francesco had proved impossible to persuade but his son had jumped at the opportunity and had been paying ever since, even when Francesco was still around and Pablo was getting himself into all sorts of trouble. MacMillan didn't like Pablo at all, but enjoyed the ten grand a month he had been earning as a retainer for the last few years. But there was a problem; the payments had stopped. MacMillan had spoken once only to Pablo about this and delivered a short and concise message; if I don't get paid, don't call me. He knew it was only a matter of time, but less than two months since his last payment he was surprised to see the message 'Home Insurance Calling' on the phone's display. Home Insurance, he knew this wouldn't escape any close investigation but it covered any casual observation when Pablo called. He was tempted to ignore it, but MacMillan had recently bought a luxury holiday home on the north coast of Mexico and his mistress wanted a new car. He also fancied a nice boat to go with his new house. He had plenty of cash stashed in various places, but wanted more. He closed his office door and answered.

'Pablo.'

'Frank.'

'I wondered how long it would take. So what, you sending my money over?'

'Yeah, yeah of course Frank. It's just been a mix up. Shit happens, you know that. Hey, listen, I got an urgent job for you.'

MacMillan wasn't going to let Pablo off the hook that easily.

'OK, well, whatever. Pay me what you owe and we'll talk.'

Back in his office Pablo bit his lip to stop himself shouting out. Skinny was back already and standing next to his desk so Pablo shooed him out the room and then adopted a more conversational tone.

'Say Frank, no problem. But this one has a special pay-out for you. Well worth your while I have to say, and it's not even gonna be difficult I swear.'

'How special?'

'Easy fifty for you.'

'Plus the twenty you owe?'

Pablo gritted his teeth.

'Yeah Frank, sure. Like I said, it's just been one of those things, I had some problems with my guys. You know how these things go.'

MacMillan considered. Seventy grand would be good, save dipping into his extremely substantial savings.

'OK Pablo, give me twenty minutes. I'll drop in.'

In the end, it was nearly an hour before MacMillan wandered into Pablo's office; he did this deliberately to make sure Pablo knew who was in charge. Pablo had spent the time getting increasingly desperate. The presence of Shaun Farley sitting waiting patiently was weighing down heavily now. Skinny had obviously just made the situation even worse when he had gone to talk, and Pablo should have known better than to ask him but he was not only desperate, but trapped in his office.

Pablo was in a mess. And now he knew it. And he was forced to admit that Stefan leaving was also taking its toll, Pablo had been relying on him for years. Stefan just always understood what to do, he had all the contacts, everybody knew him and he appreciated how things worked. In truth while he had often been hard on the men they had working for them there had really been very little trouble, and Pablo had been well protected from the many people out there looking for money. Now, Stefan was out, Robert and Jimmy were in hospital and it looked like Tony was probably going to join them, there was no news at all where he could be. That only left Skinny, who was there like a bad smell hovering around the office.

Watching Frank MacMillan belligerently stroll into his office Pablo knew he couldn't display any of his true feelings. He suddenly became aware of his appearance and affected an air of someone who had been living it up.

'Mac!' he declared cheerfully.

MacMillan looked at him carefully, immediately sensing problems. In truth, there were a lot of rumours circulating about Pablo, as usual MacMillan was keen to avoid anything that could be even remotely inconvenient. He noticed the absence of Stefan and made an elaborate show of looking around, completely ignoring Skinny.

'Hey. So where's Stefan at?'

Pablo dismissively waved a hand.

'That fucker. Who knows and who cares? I've been carrying that loser too long, he's outta here.'

This was a real shock to MacMillan. Stefan was the only reason Pablo was still alive and everyone knew it; he was streetwise, smart, cool and capable. Everything Pablo wasn't.

'So what, you're running things on your own now?' MacMillan was incredulous.

Skinny went to speak but Pablo quietened him patiently.

'Everything is just fine Mac. No problem.'

'Well, I'm hearing things Pablo.'

'Yeah? What things?' Pablo retorted angrily.

'You're broke. You got some heavy people on your case. And you got no team left. I'm thinking, no way, not Pablo. But then I ain't getting paid, and seeing as Stefan is not here, I'm wondering what the real story is. Make no mistake Pablo, I know you got shit going down. Everybody knows.

'Trust me Mac, there's no problem. And fuck all those other guys, they can say what they want. It's just jealousy is what it is.'

Pablo kept the smile on his face, but inside he was in turmoil. Who was talking about him? How many people knew about his money problems, or New York? He couldn't think of a single person he could turn to other than Mac, and here the policeman was making him feel like trash and bringing up gossip. But he needed the money back, and there was only one way he could think of to make it happen.

MacMillan sighed and sat down.

'OK, well … I guess I'm here now. Tell me what you need Pablo.'

Pablo took out the photo of John Smith taken at the immigration desk and laid it out on the desk. MacMillan picked it up and looked at it. He didn't recognise the man, who at best looked nondescript.

'So?'

'So I need this guy found. He's stolen a lot of money from me.'

'Who is he?'

'His name's John Smith. He's a Brit. He's over here to take me down. Today he robbed two of my guys, I got this other guy waiting to get paid, it's all very fucking boring but I need it dealt with. It's a respect thing you understand.'

'No, not really. Why would a British guy come over here to get you?'

'There's a disagreement over some fucking money. I didn't feel like paying so hey, I didn't. It's bullshit.'

But suddenly a light came on in MacMillan's mind, something he had been told in the last couple of days that he didn't really take a lot of notice of, but now rang a loud alarm in his brain. He smiled at Pablo.

'Whoa, wait a second. Hold up. This is the guy right? People are saying he took out that fucking giant Robert at McCarran? This is what I been hearing. This guy? And now he's stealing off you?'

'Look Mac, yeah OK he's been giving me some problems. I don't know, I never met him. From what I found out he's like some fucking Special Forces martial arts expert or some shit. But I need the fucker found, I need that money back.'

But MacMillan was weighing everything up. He wasn't sure at all that he wanted any part of this. This guy, whoever he was, had to be trouble. Robert was big. There were bigger out there sure, but Robert had been around, he'd been putting the squeeze on people a long time.

'I don't know I want to do this Pablo. OK, so why don't you just go talk to him? Avoid any more problems.'

'We don't know where he's staying. He made reservations at half the hotels on the strip, checked in at all of them but from what we know he never stepped foot in any of the rooms.'

MacMillan shook his head and sat there silently, thinking. He really didn't like the sound of this at all.

'Pablo, let me give you some advice. You don't have to listen of course, but I think you should.'

Pablo sat back and shrugged, as usual never willing to listen to any suggestions and conscious of time passing.

'Look Pablo, just hear me out for Christ's sakes, there is every chance that this is not just some guy, right? I mean Robert? Come on. And this hotel stunt? I never heard of that before. And now he's taking on more of your guys? You got any left apart from this fat idiot?'

Skinny jumped and stared, but MacMillan ignored him.

'Mac, listen …' Pablo blustered but was interrupted.

'Hear me out. You know what? However this started, get out of it. Just pay the fucking guy! Then forget about it. OK, so you didn't pay and he's come after you, but now he's got the money back right? Maybe with some cream on the top. But I can tell you something and you need to listen to this, you are not looking at a guy you walk away from. Understand what he does. What he is. This is his job, and it sounds like he's good at it. You got nobody left Pablo. Nobody, even Stefan has bailed.'

'Mac, it's not that simple. OK, between me and you, I got a minor cashflow problem.'

Skinny looked surprised, but MacMillan had already worked out all the rumours are true as soon as he came in the room.

'All the more reason Pablo. And by the way, this ain't a mystery, people are saying you got money problems, and from what I am hearing, it ain't so minor. Everybody knows you're broke, everybody. But you got to open your ears; with this John Smith you need to let it go, the guy will just keep coming. To me, it looks like you're gonna lose, and lose bad.'

'Bullshit Mac. I never lose.'

MacMillan stood and stared at Pablo, who looked anywhere else. He was a mess.

'You ain't listening Pablo. Everybody is talking. You've been losing a long, long time.'

Pablo cleared his throat.

'Mac, I need that money back, and I need it today.'

'You're making a mistake Pablo.'

'I ain't got any choices any more Mac.'

MacMillan sighed.

'OK, so what do you want me to do?'

'Simple, find him, take him in, and get my money.'

'It doesn't sound that simple. This is a big city. What do I arrest him for? Robert ain't gonna testify and I guess you don't want this money discussed.'

'Whatever you want. Car theft, he stole one of ours, it's in the lot. I don't fucking know, just find him.'

MacMillan stood still and considered. The cash would be handy, and he would be able to make sure he got it. He should be able to find Smith, it wouldn't be difficult for him to mobilise a bunch of cops out with the photo. He had to be staying somewhere, someone must have seen him. Start with the strip; it was the most likely place. Pablo looked at him anxiously. MacMillan took out his phone and called the precinct ordering some crime scene guys to come down and fingerprint the car.

'OK. Pay me my twenty right now, and I want a hundred for the job. And don't try and argue.'

'Deal.' Pablo replied simply. He sent Skinny off to the cashier's office. He could replace the money later; Shaun would just have to take two million after all.

Chapter Thirteen

John and George had a very late lunch at the country club while discussing the next move. John was keen to hit Honeys and speak to Thomas, but George advised him to leave it until later, there would be nobody there other than some booze hounds until the evening, and if Thomas was working there then it was more likely that he would be around then.

'So where you staying?' George suddenly asked.

'Venetian,' John lied automatically.

'Why you really doing this John?'

'I told you, I'm looking for Abby.'

'I get that, but if I had to guess this is your job right? You ain't just a friend of the family, and if you are then lucky them. You're just too good at this. You've done this before. I got no problem with it, it's obvious that you know what the hell you're doing, but I like to know where I stand.'

John paused and stared at George, who looked back with an interested expression on his face. John shrugged.

'Yeah. I'm getting paid.'

'So this is what you do?'

'Among other things.'

'John, I'm just asking. It ain't my business. You're a gun for hire.'

'No, I'm not that.'

'OK, I'll shut the fuck up.'

John sighed.

'OK, OK. It's no problem. Yeah, I find people. I sort out problems. I settle scores; get debts paid, that sort of thing.'

'And I'm guessing you're real good at it. I watched you my friend, I never seen anyone so calm. You never even broke a sweat. John I got to say you could be very useful, my contacts in New York would be real interested, and it would be very worth your while.'

John smiled.

'Thanks George, but I'm happy doing what I do. I'm not bothered about money, never have been. And I like where I live.'

'OK. Well, you got a bunch more money sitting in the trunk of my car.'

Both men laughed.

'That is true George.'

'By the way John, I got a good way to get that cash out the picture. I'd consider it a personal favour if we get it moved like yesterday. The longer it's around, the more poisonous it could get, and I need to keep it distant. It never existed. And Pablo's crew, if he's even got one now, well they are gonna be looking for you.'

'OK, sure, what do we do?'

'Take it to UPS! Seriously, I got a good guy at the airport. It will be all packed up and gone, waiting for you when you get home with no trace anywhere. And far away from here, which is all I care about.'

'Sounds like a plan, thanks George. But you know I'm not worried about them looking for me.'

'The game has changed now. Pablo's got no choice, he is gonna have to try real hard, he's got cops on the payroll.'

'Oh yeah? Do you know who?'

'This old sweat lieutenant or whatever Frank MacMillan definitely. He used to pay off the DA and this captain over at Metro, but they got busted over corruption a few years ago. Department is supposedly squeaky clean now but MacMillan is still there, on the take, and not just off Pablo. I don't know him, never met the guy but he's been steering things in this city a long time. My guess is Pablo will set the dogs loose, but as I said earlier he's run out of friends. If you need a wingman with MacMillan let me know, it would be a pleasure.'

'George I got one more question, I read in a file about the FBI investigating, and Eddie mentioned them too. Why didn't that stick? Rapes, murders, guns, drugs? There must have been a pile of evidence a mile high.'

'I asked myself the same question, and Francesco won't answer it either. He just won't talk about it. It must have been a pay-off, someone must have got a slice of the pie.'

'If you're serious about getting Francesco out, I think you need them to look at it again.'

'Yeah? Tell me something I don't know. But how in hell am I supposed to get that done? I avoid those guys John, I've spent my life doing it. I don't know about you.'

'Once I find out what happened to Abby, either way that comes out I am out of here. But I do know someone, and they owe me. I could give them a call, but I don't want to bring any heat down on anyone that would cause you a problem if you see what I mean.'

George said nothing, considering. He made his mind up.

'I can hardly believe I'm talking about this. I've never had any direct dealings with those guys, and that's how I like it. Just say I agree, and I would try anything for Francesco, how well do you know this guy? This could blow wide open, I got a lot of friends with business interests in the Acropolis as you know, and these guys do not like to have their names known believe me.'

'The guy owes me. He is high enough up to make decisions. I don't think I can tell him everything but I can certainly ask him to be careful. I think if I word it carefully and explain what I need to he'll understand. It may not be in his interests to dig too deep because it could distract from everything else. I'm sure I can get the message across.'

'Do it. For Francesco. But for Christ's sakes let me know what's going on.'

They left the country club and John followed George out to the airport to a UPS shipping office. George was treated like an old friend, some cash from the ten grand John got on his first day changed hands, and the bag containing two and a half million dollars was packed in an official looking plastic crate and sealed. It was marked as sensitive material and sent to a postal address which John had the use of when needed.

Once that was done it was already full dark. John dropped the Mustang back at the Avis desk and then travelled back to the strip with George and got out at the Venetian. He arranged to call later and walked into the hotel.

Once inside he walked through and down into the shopping area, then looped around back out onto the strip. He moved as quickly and discretely as he could through the crowds, grateful for the tip off from George. He noticed that there were cops everywhere, it seemed like many more than before, but that could just be because he was looking out for them rather than the other way round.

He crossed the strip down past Flamingo, and continued walking, in and out of hotels and shops, then through New York New York, then Excalibur, entered the Luxor and used the link to cross into the Mandalay Bay, then circled round and then crossed back through the casino, always moving, always looking around. As he went through the bar the pretty blonde barmaid stopped him.

'Cops are looking for you Mr Smith,' she told him with a wide smile.

John affected a look of surprise.

'Oh yeah? Why would that be I wonder?'

'No idea. They didn't say much, just showing your picture. I said I hadn't seen you. Didn't know you.'

'Thank you. Thank you very much.'

'Come down later, you can buy me a drink. Thank me properly.'

She gave him a look and then walked away. John watched her go. A drink with her later would be very good.

He made it back to his suite without incident, and removed the remaining Glock. He packed it along with the other guns and ammo, his alternate ID's and the wig into the holdall which had originally held the money. He called George who answered straight away.

'George, you're right. I got the police out and about looking for me.'

'That figures. Pablo doesn't like to do anything for himself. He got nobody else to do it now anyhow.'

'Well, I'm thinking I may as well find out why.'

'You sure?'

'Oh yeah, I've been here before. Getting set up is part of the game, but it's not one I've lost so far. It'll be OK. Can you get me a brief?'

'Yeah, probably. What the hell is a brief?'

John laughed out loud.

'A solicitor, an attorney.'

'Oh yeah, I can do that no problem. Yeah I see what you're saying. I can get someone with you in a couple of hours latest. It'll be the south precinct; Metro is cleaned up, least that's what everyone is saying so it won't be no good to Pablo anymore, and anyway that's where MacMillan is based.'

'OK, well I'll make my way there. Listen George, I want to get all this sorted out tonight if I can; I got to find Abby, good or bad. I really don't wanna get stuck in a cell for hours on end, so tell him whatever you need to.'

'It's a her, but yeah. I get it. She'll know the situation.'

'George I need to get Pablo out the way. I don't mean like you think I mean, but I need to get rid of him and you might not like what I'm going to do, but like I said before I am going to do all I can to limit the damage. I'm getting a bad feeling now about Abby, and all the time he's around it's causing me a problem.'

'Do what you got to do.'

'Thanks George, I'll be in touch.'

John sent a text, and then sat looking out the window waiting for a response. Ten minutes later his phone rang.

'John.'

'Hello.'

'What can I do for you?'

'I need work, home and mobile numbers for Special Agent Patrick Skelton. FBI. He's a supervisor or something like that. Last I knew he's based in Washington.'

'No problem. We'll get back to you.'

'Thanks.'

John hung the phone up. He looked out the window at the Acropolis and flicked the television on to pass the time. The Simpsons was on, where Homer becomes an astronaut. It was one of his favourite episodes, had to be a good sign.

Twenty minutes later as the credits were rolling his phone beeped. A concise message with three phone numbers. He decided to try the office phone first.

Chapter Fourteen

Special Agent Patrick Skelton was looking out the window of his office when the phone rang. In Washington, the temperature had really dropped, he could see trees bending in the strong winds and rain was bouncing high off the roofs of parked cars. Everywhere he looked headlights were crawling along in both directions. He was mulling over the best way to get home as the traffic was only going to get worse and twirling a pen in his left hand. He grabbed the phone up with his right and rocked back in his chair.

'Yeah?'

'I have a John Smith for you.'

Patrick dropped the pen on the desk with a clatter and sat up straight staring at the phone in shock. John Smith!!!! There was a name that he had believed he would never hear again. It had been what, more than five years? Longer? It was a period that he tried to put out of his mind, it was not a good memory. He had been working down in Atlanta on a relatively routine investigation which had suddenly spiralled out of control without warning. An agent was shot and killed getting out of a car in a hotel car park and then Patrick had been grabbed and bundled into a van by three men while he was on surveillance; sitting on his own in an all night fast food place watching out the window at a storage depot on the other side of the road. Due to the sudden escalation they were short on bodies and he had been working for over twenty-four hours straight. He didn't take it in when the men came in to the restaurant and had been tied up with plastic ties and blindfolded. He bounced around in the back of a van for half an hour or so and then was dragged into a vacant old building and locked in a large store room. He had no idea where he was or who had taken him. He was left for a few hours then two men came in and ripped off the blindfold. He knew he didn't have long left when they made no effort to hide their faces. He was thrown around the room and beaten; they were asking questions about the investigation and demanding details on what information he had. Patrick did what he could trying to buy time while knowing for sure he would be killed anyway. Just as it was getting serious they got a call on a cell phone, and they left him alone again. He was sitting on the floor bleeding when suddenly the door opened and John Smith was thrown in, similarly bound but also without the blindfold.

As soon as the door shut, John Smith wasted no time. Explaining to Patrick they were basically on the same side but running out of time fast he prowled around the room, searching. Eventually he spotted something and laid down on the floor flat on his back, and after some exertion the plastic tie snapped holding his arms. Free, he made short work of the two men's remaining ties and then began hammering on the door.

Patrick recovered enough to try to take charge but it was fruitless, Smith was like a well-oiled machine moving rapidly in only one direction. He indicated for Patrick to stand in front and then went to the side, hidden when the door was flung open. One of the men came in cursing loudly and holding a gun, which he pushed into Patrick's temple as he walked through the door. In less than a few seconds somehow Smith had it in his hand, and the man was out cold with two broken arms and smashed hands. They went through the building side by side, disarming everyone they met, almost ridiculously easily. Smith just knew what to do at every obstacle they came across and dealt with everything methodically. He seemed to hardly have a scratch on him. They recovered Patrick's belongings, and as Smith handed over the FBI badge he stated politely that he was never there and ran from the building. Still in shock Patrick agreed and gratefully called the cavalry.

As quickly as he had arrived, John Smith had vanished.

He owed Smith not only his life, but also the medal he won for valour and the promotion for bringing down a major people trafficking ring. John Smith was one man that he was never going to forget.

But now Patrick couldn't very well believe this being a social call, and his immediate thought was to avoid it; Smith could want absolutely anything. He could have been sitting in a room somewhere plotting for the last five years. But then the memories of his despair at being locked in the room and the desperate thoughts of his family entered his head, and he answered.

'Patrick?'

'Jesus Christ John, I thought I had dreamt you!'

'No, no Patrick I'm real enough. Thanks for taking my call.'

'It's been a long time John. And I never really got to thank you. Nobody did.'

'It has been a long time and just forget about it, as far as I can see we helped each other.'

'So are you in town? You want to meet?'

'No, it's not that. I think I've got something you might be interested in, but it needs to be fast. Really fast. Tonight.'

Patrick wondered where this was going; he still couldn't work out whether John was looking for some kind of a favour; money even.

'OK John, I'm listening.'

Carefully John explained the situation in Las Vegas. Starting with Francesco, and then Pablo, and ending where they were right now and also telling Patrick that he was only really there looking for Abby.

'I got kinda caught up in it to be honest Patrick. It's not really my business, but I can't help it if I get dragged in. But then I found out you guys had already been involved in the past anyway, and I got kind of confused about why it never led to anything if I'm honest. It's clear as day that this Pablo is no good, I can't imagine any way that your guys on the ground could have missed it.'

While he was listening, Patrick logged on to his computer and began running through the names on his computer; something that he did every working day. There was a whole lot of files from 2005 onwards, which then suddenly ended. It had been handled by the FBI's Las Vegas field office as he had expected. But as he quickly scanned through the files straight away he could see that something had been done to the records, one agent would file a report, next another would file word for word the same, and another, all within hours of each other then there would be no follow up. Something stank. The whole thing looked like a five year olds writing project.

'I'll tell you what John. I'm looking at the Escola files right now. And I have to say, this isn't making a whole lot of sense to me either. You say this needs to be fast, what do you mean?

'Well I think I'm getting close to Abby, hopefully still alive, and I've been doing a lot of damage to the organisation down here.'

Patrick could well imagine.

'So are you saying that there may not be a case soon?'

'No, I'm saying that I think Pablo Escola is about to run. And that will leave his father on Death Row, every chance of a dead girl and a whole lot of people out of pocket.'

'OK. John, let me read through all this stuff properly and get hold of some people and call you back. It could be a few hours. Is that OK with you?

'As long as it's tonight that's fine. Thanks Patrick.'

'OK John, talk soon.'

'And Patrick, please be careful. There are some not so innocent people on the edges of this I could do without upsetting.'

'Not so innocent?'

'Look, if you could avoid looking too deeply into the hotel itself; especially the owners I would appreciate it. I probably don't need to spell it out, but I've been getting some help, and I don't want to cause anyone any trouble.'

Patrick sighed. Things were never simple, but he understood exactly what John was asking.

'I hear you.'

John went downstairs and left the hotel. He walked south past the aquarium and toward the golf club. There was a line of bushes and he followed them along to a lamp post and wedged the bag deep inside, then he returned to Reception and asked where the police station was.

Pablo's phone rang; he saw it was Frank MacMillan calling. That was fast he thought gratefully as he hadn't moved since MacMillan left; he was still in his office hiding from Shaun Farley. Pablo had been trying to revive a relationship he had from years before; a contact who had supplied a lot of cocaine in another of Pablo's failed enterprises. But it had been cash on delivery, so no money was owed and the man was out the way; down in San Diego. Pablo was thinking he would do well to get out of town, for a while at least. So far, the conversation had not been too enthusiastic, so he was very happy to get the call.

'Mac?'

'Pablo, it's Smith. He's here.'

'Wow that was quick Mac! What, not even two hours. Shit. My guys have been looking for two days and no sign anywhere.'

'We didn't find him. That's why I'm calling. He walked in Pablo. On his own. Right through the front door.'

The phone hung up and Pablo stared at it dumbly.

Smith had just turned up at the police station?

What the hell did that mean?

Chapter Fifteen

John sat in an interview room, there was a uniformed officer standing just outside the open door. He checked his watch; ten past nine. This was a gamble that could backfire; he didn't want to get stuck here but it was important that Pablo and any corrupt cops knew he wasn't going to be intimidated. He was well aware the police had nothing on him; this was nothing more than a tactic to scare him and find the money. So he didn't need to worry about that, he just had to avoid being detained for too long. He looked out the window; he could see sporadic traffic on the road behind the police station and intermittent rain pattering lightly on the glass.

He heard voices outside and a woman wearing a smart business suit entered the room. She was in her early forties and attractive, holding herself in a 'I am way out of your league' kind of way. John liked her immediately.

'Hello John, I'm Helen Greengrove. Your attorney.'

'Hi Helen, good to meet you.'

They shook hands then Helen walked over and ignoring the officer outside pushed the door shut firmly.

John gave her a brief rundown; the police were looking for him, he hadn't done anything and George had offered to help.

She nodded. Clearly she had been given some details and it was obvious she already knew exactly who and what George was.

'No problem John. How long have you been here?'

'In this room? Maybe twenty minutes, but I've been in this station for a couple of hours now. Maybe a bit longer. George said you'd be a while which is fine, no problem at all but I could do with getting out really.'

'Two hours? Right.'

She jumped up, then walked out pulling the door open and demanded a senior officer attend immediately, or John would leave. The cop outside was immediately out of his depth and scurried off. A sergeant appeared and started to tell her about ongoing investigations in progress but she cut him down.

'You have three minutes. If a senior officer is not here before then we will leave. Mr Smith is not a US citizen and is therefore allowed the full courtesy offered by International law. He has committed no crime and came here of his own accord. He has done nothing wrong, and yet has been held here for over two hours. Every second late he is waiting while you attempt to get him to stay after the three minutes are up I will personally ensure that he earns the same in hourly compensation. I advise that you do not doubt my word.'

She returned into the room, smiled widely at John, sat down and crossed her legs.

Less than three minutes later Lieutenant Frank MacMillan entered the room and took a seat opposite them. The officer from outside followed him in and closed the door, standing to one side.

'Ah, Lieutenant MacMillan. The one and only,' Helen said sardonically. 'You still have a job then? That's amazing, congratulations.'

MacMillan pursed his lips then forced a tight smile.

'Ms Greengrove, Mr Smith.'

Helen wasted no time.

'I'd like to know what the hell is going here Lieutenant MacMillan. Mr Smith is here on vacation. He is wasting his time seated in a police station after coming here of his own volition and has been here over two hours. I am very unhappy about his treatment.'

'Why did you come here Mr Smith?' MacMillan asked; totally unsure of the situation but at least trying to be business-like.

'This police station? Civic duty I suppose. I heard the police were looking for me.'

'No Mr Smith, not the police precinct, why here. Las Vegas.'

'I'm looking for someone. Abby Cromwell.'

'What's that, a missing person? That's a PD matter Mr Smith, whoever she is.'

'That's exactly what I said. But I was asked to come regardless and actually I think I'm very close to finding her now.'

'OK, So ... what was the reason that you came to the police precinct.'

'Because when I got back to my hotel I was told the police had called and were looking for me.'

MacMillan nodded slowly.

'Which hotel is that? Where are you staying?'

'Bellagio, room twenty-seventeen,' John lied smoothly in return with a smile.

MacMillan turned to the officer and asked him to check that.

'Lieutenant, perhaps you can explain why you were looking for Mr Smith and why you deem it necessary to find out where he is staying?' Helen was clearly ready for a fight.

'Ms Greengrove, there has been an allegation of car theft against Mr Smith.'

Car theft? John hadn't expected that. Interesting.

'I see. And what car is this?'

'A dark blue Lincoln Navigator. The property of the Acropolis Hotel. A complaint was made, we have to investigate. I'm sure you understand.'

Helen sat back, and looked at John, who shrugged and smiled.

'No idea,' he told her.

'Lieutenant, I assume you have evidence of this?'

'We are waiting for a full report from the examiner.'

'OK, so you must have witnesses who have seen Mr Smith steal the car, or even drive it?'

MacMillan kept quiet, buying time.

The officer returned and spoke in MacMillan's ear. The lieutenant pursed his lips.

John Smith was registered and checked in at the Bellagio, room twenty-seventeen. That asshole Pablo, he couldn't do anything right. The guy was right in front of him.

Helen heard every word and tapped her fingernails on the desk impatiently.

'In that case lieutenant, I assume then that Mr Smith is free to go?'

MacMillan said nothing in reply, turning instead to John.

'Mr Smith, I have to ask, if you are here looking for this person, in an unofficial capacity, then surely you would have contacted the police in the city on arrival? And now you are here, as an innocent party who has done nothing wrong, why would you wish to engage an attorney? Especially one as expensive and Miss Greengrove.'

'Oh, I was really shocked to hear the police were looking for me. It was quite upsetting actually. So I spoke to a friend I have here. He suggested it would be a good idea, I don't understand the law you see, I have very little to do with it.'

'I see. And what friend was that?'

'Oh it's Pablo. Pablo Escola. He owns the Acropolis actually. So I am rather surprised about all of this I have to say.'

MacMillan stared at John. That was clever, too clever. What did this guy know? Jesus Christ, he could know everything! Helen gave nothing away, she continued to look at him.

There was a tap at the door, and the officer opened it. He was given a sheet of paper which he passed to MacMillan.

MacMillan read it, but had already guessed the content.

There was not one single fingerprint belonging to John Smith in the Lincoln.

He stood up and fixed a smile to his face.

'Mr Smith, clearly this has been a mistake. I am very sorry to have held you up. Sometimes we are given misleading information, and I apologise on behalf of the Las Vegas PD.'

'Lieutenant?' Helen looked enquiringly at him.

'Er ... yes Ms Greengrove?'

'I notice that none of this is being recorded. So, I assume

that as Mr Smith is here on his own volition this entire episode has been a waste of all our time?'

MacMillan coughed.

'Again, I apologise Mr Smith. Please enjoy the rest of your stay in our city, you are free to go.'

Without bothering to pick up the report MacMillan left the room.

Up in his office he called Pablo back and broke the news.

'I'm telling you Mac, he is not staying at the Bellagio'

'Pablo how exactly do you know this? You been over there yourself?'

'Cos I have had guys watching out for him.'

'Guys? You got nobody left.'

'Whatever. This ain't helping. What are you doing about this Mac?'

'I can't do anything. He hasn't broken any laws. Helen Greengrove was in there with him, biggest ball-breaker in this city and she is already causing me enough problems as you well know.'

'Well, you put a tail on him right? He will lead us to the money!'

'Pablo, this ain't the movies. No, I ain't put a tail on him. I got nothing, there ain't a single goddamn print in the car and he has a valid address which has been checked out by us and confirmed at the hotel. The captain is already gonna be looking real close at this, Ms Helen fucking Greengrove will see to that. This is no good Pablo, I cannot be in the spotlight. I gotta stay away.'

Pablo's voice raised a few octaves higher.

'Mac you got to do something! Listen to me I need your help. You got to keep on him and find my fucking money!'

'Pablo, he'll turn up. I don't think he's finished with you yet. He's saying the reason he's here is he's gotta find that fucking Abby, and Christ alone knows what the fuck you done with her. It's got nothing to do with money or any of your bullshit. He's connected Abby to you and it's my guess is he'll be coming to see you, and I get the feeling it won't be long.'

'That's not helping!' Pablo squeaked.

'You know what he did Pablo? He told me you recommended Helen fucking Greengrove; said you were old pals. This guy is way too smart; and I know that means he's most likely heading for a fall, but no way am I taking a chance. If I were you I would get everybody you got around you and just keep watching out; you could get lucky, maybe, but I'm done. No more Pablo, no more.'

'Mac! Listen. Fuck! I need ...'

MacMillan saw the captain in the corridor and hurriedly hung up the phone, switching it off completely.

In his office Pablo stared down at the phone in his hand, and redialled. It went straight to voicemail. He threw the phone across the room and buried his head in his hands. He was a prisoner, he couldn't leave the room in case he ran into Shaun Farley. His office was right in the centre of the ground floor administration area, there were no windows and outside his door was just a bland corridor, which led one way to the lift up to the penthouse and the other back to the hotel. He was totally cut off. He had no idea of what to do next. Abby. John Smith was over here looking for her. He should have thought of that. All this shit could easily have been avoided. But it wasn't his fault. He had been given bad information and worse advice.

He sat there, perilously close to tears for the first time in many years then stood up, crossed the room and locked the door. Slowly he crawled around collecting the bits of the mobile phone and clipping them back together.

He needed help, but there was nobody out there. Nobody at all.

He needed to think. Maybe John Smith was staying at the Bellagio but Pablo didn't have any friends there; Stefan had been the one with the connections. Pablo realised he should have done something, anything to keep Stefan. He had been a rock for years, and now Pablo really was on his own, he couldn't rely on Skinny to get a cup of coffee without a detailed list of instructions and even then, it would most likely be screwed up. He could of course walk over to the Bellagio himself, but knew he would not be welcome there, plus that would put him back out in the hotel where Shaun Farley was apparently still waiting. Skinny had not done a good job at all of persuading him that everything was fine.

Now, the fact that he didn't know what to do was bearing down on him, hard. The money had gone, the only person he knew that had any chance of getting it back had let him down. He picked up the mobile and scrolled down to Stefan then dialled.

He would make peace; Stefan would know what to do.

A phone shrilled on his desk, he looked around and then stared down at it dumbly and remembered then that Stefan had given the mobile back. He hung up.

He was completely on his own.

Chapter Sixteen

Once he left the police station John thanked Helen Greengrove and went into overdrive. He walked north, went back to the strip and entered the MGM Grand from the rear, then circled around it several times and exited from the same door, before re-entering and emerging back onto the strip where he crossed the road, went back on himself and entered Excalibur, then circled round the casino before using the footbridge to access New York New York. He carried on making his way up the strip, criss-crossing the busy road and merging with the crowds, entering and leaving the hotels until he walked through the Wynn and caught the monorail at the Convention Centre.

He knew for sure he wasn't being followed. It was raining gently and in the warmth of the Las Vegas evening it was pleasant.

He got out at SLS and then headed east, sticking to the side roads until he saw the rear of Honeys. He crossed the car park and walked around the building to the front door then wandered in.

It was busier than the last time, but still not exactly jumping. The music was loud; a US soft rock band playing and a girl was disinterestedly gyrating around a pole on the stage. There were men scattered around sitting at the tables, singly or in small groups. There was nobody at the greeter station but the fat man was behind the bar, along with another much younger man. John looked around carefully, there was no sign of Thomas.

John sat down at the bar and ordered a beer from the young barman, looking around the room. There was a corridor leading off the back with toilets on either side of it, and then a fire exit at the end. There was another two doors further along the wall, maybe one of them was an office?

The fat barman kept looking at him, trying to work out if he knew him. He was wearing a red cowboy shirt with an oval name badge bearing the name 'Ron'. John ignored him. It was clear that the guys seated at the bar around were regulars, passing occasional comments between themselves. One of them, a thin guy with glasses kept laughing at everything Ron said.

The act ended to scattered applause and a new girl appeared on the stage, Velvet Revolver started playing 'Slither', which was one of his favourite songs.

John took a swig of his beer and caught the young bartender's eye.

'So, Thomas around?' he asked.

Ron's head snapped up and he stared at John with narrow eyes. He slammed up the bar counter flap and walked around to stand right next to John, who remained seated and took another drink.

'I knew I recognised you. Nosy fucker. I told you to fuck off before and I'm saying it again. Fuck off or you'll see what you get.'

John put his beer bottle down slowly and carefully on the bar and turned in his seat and looked at Ron impassively.

'What'll I get then Ron?'

Ron face turned darker red.

'I was nice last time. But you only get that once. So let's step outside and I'll show you, fuckface.'

John finished his beer and stood up and leaned in close to Ron and patted him on the cheek.

'So let's go,' he told him with a grin and walked out the door.

'You want a piece of this Stevo? Ron called out to the thin guy with the glasses who jumped up and they both followed John outside.

John walked across to the pavement and turned to face the door as the two other men emerged; Ron leading the way with Stevo grinning away behind him. It was raining heavier now, there were a few people around; most were heading in the direction of the strip. He watched the two men as they came down the steps and moved forward to meet them. Ron was the tough guy, but out of shape. Muscle turned to flab, probably at one time he had been more than capable in a scrap. There was nothing to Stevo other than skin, bone and the start of a pot belly from beer. He was staying back, grinning, confident that he could safely watch Ron smack the British guy around and afterwards he could take some credit for the backup. Probably a beer on the house.

'I didn't come here for this,' John told Ron as they closed in.

'I bet you fucking didn't. You'll be real sorry you set foot in my place.'

The music was blasting through the open doors behind them.

Ron moved forward, 'I'm gonna ....'

But John interrupted him, holding up a hand.

'Wait, this is my favourite bit, the solo is about to start,' he said.

And bizarrely Ron stopped dead, a confused look on his face.

The music paused, and then Slash let rip, shredding the notes to a crescendo, the final sustain ringing out.

All the time John stood still, listening attentively, while Ron just stared at him, his frown getting deeper.

'Thanks,' John smiled.

'You motherfucker, I'm gonna tear you apart,' Ron moved forward again.

John waited until they were less than a metre apart and then suddenly glanced over Ron's shoulder, widening his eyes as he did so.

It was way too easy.

Instinctively Ron turned his head to glance over his shoulder and that was all John needed.

Leaning into his left he threw a solid right hander which caught Ron squarely across the side of his jaw, instantly breaking it. Ron let out a muffled sigh and fell forward. Still moving John kicked out hard and connected solidly with the other man's knee, causing the leg to buckle and as Ron fell he kicked out again catching him under the chin.

Ron's eyes rolled up in his head and he crashed to the wet ground out cold. In panic Stevo turned heading for the safety of the bar but John grabbed the back of his shirt and pulled him back, then threw him onto the ground next to Ron.

'Please!' Stevo exclaimed wildly staring at John and holding his hands upward, rain speckling his glasses.

John leaned in close and sat him up.

'Look after Ron. Don't disappoint me,' he told him and walked back into the bar.

With a nod to the remaining barman who now looked extremely confused John walked around the bar heading for the two doors at the rear of the place. The first one was locked, presumably a store room of some kind so he pulled open the second and walked into a small office, with just a desk, chair and a filing cabinet inside.

Thomas was seated behind the desk, with a bottle of whisky in front of him. He looked up startled, and then a look of resignation came over his face.

'Ah,' he said as John leaned on the doorframe in front of him.

'We need to have a talk.' John told him.

Thomas poured himself a generous measure of the whisky.

'Well ... you see ...' he replied desperately, then drank down the whole thing.

'Let's go somewhere else,' John said patiently.

Thomas played with the glass in front of him and then sighed.

'Yes. Alright.'

They left Honeys, outside Stevo had Ron sitting up and was trying to clean his face. Thomas stopped and looked down, scratching his head, bewildered. John threw a five dollar bill on the ground next to Ron.

'I never paid for that beer.'

They walked along past two blocks in silence. Thomas appeared to know where he was going and they entered a small, quiet shabby bar with a huge 'Welcome to Vegas' sign in the window. Thomas seemed to know the people working behind the counter and raised two fingers as he entered, then sat down in a booth at the side.

John sat opposite and a man shuffled over and put two whiskies down on the table.

Thomas immediately scooped one up.

'Cheers,' he muttered and took a sip.

Thomas was short and slim, with a careworn look about him. Meeting him in the flesh John decided that all the suspicions about him and Abby were unlikely. He was hardly a catch. John leaned forward and looked at Thomas intently.

'Hasn't worked out has it?' he asked.

Thomas looked away and shook his head.

'No. And I can't go back. I've fucked up and I know it.'

'So go on then, why? Because of Abby?'

Thomas looked surprised to be asked, and then shrugged.

'She played me, of course she did. Got me to bring her out here. Daddy wasn't happy about it, said no to her for once so she sought me out. She was good at that. Manipulative. I was thinking that maybe she was interested. But Pablo treated her like royalty, so it was over before it began for me. If it ever was going to of course. Now, she doesn't even speak to me, and I'm not exactly high on the food chain.'

'She came out here to be with Pablo?'

'Not at first. I set up here and she wanted to come out, kept emailing me. It was my fault, I introduced them. Pablo was immediately all over her, calling her his English rose. They fell in love, left me high and dry.'

'And now you're working at Honeys?'

Thomas miserably downed the rest of his drink. John gestured to him to have the other one and he reached for it gratefully.

'I had a good life with Richard. Really good, but I was always behind the scenes, the faceless nobody. And that was the point. Pablo offered me excitement, the chance to be a big man, to work the stones operation for him.'

'So you stole the money.'

'No, whatever I did, that's not true at all. Pablo never paid for the diamonds. There was a system Francesco set up, payments had to be made and the stones was the best way to do it. Avoided big amounts of cash appearing and he put it all together with Richard. But I never stole anything. Yeah, technically I was working for Richard but what else was I going to do? I was spending all my time over here. It was like paradise. I loved it. Pablo promised me the world once Francesco left.'

Thomas shook his head morosely.

'And I fell for it. I never should have done it. At first, I had everything. Nice apartment, car, and then this big blow out happened with his dad. Francesco. And next thing there's no money.'

John was taken aback.

'What do you mean?'

'His dad. He went to prison, owed a fortune. Pablo has spent the last couple of years trying to pay everyone off but then it got to the point where there was nothing left. He told me all about it, explained why there was nothing there for me.'

John rubbed his eye and counted to ten.

'Thomas, how old are you?'

'What? I'm fifty-five. What's that got to do with anything?'

'You're a bit old for fairy stories I would have said.'

Thomas shook his head.

'You're like the others. Pablo confided in me. It's just a matter of time. And he told me all about you, all about Richard getting heavy.'

'Yeah. That sound like Richard to you? You really believe that he would send me over here to get paid? And you are telling me you seriously believed the fact that Pablo is skint is down to his father? The man who built the hotel in the first place?'

'Pablo explained everything. There are massive debts everywhere. He's doing what he can.'

John gave up. What did he care about Thomas anyway?

'Thomas, where's Abby?'

'Abby? What do you want her for?'

'That's why I'm here. Richard is worried about her; he's not interested in the money. When did you last see her?'

Thomas looked surprised.

'I haven't seen her for a while, why?'

'I need to find her Thomas. As I said, that's why I'm here.'

'Well she'll be at the penthouse, with Pablo. They're getting married. Pablo told me.'

Thomas finished the second drink and looked hopefully at John, who had heard enough. Thomas and Honeys deserved each other, so let him get on with it. He stood up and threw ten dollars on the table.

'I better go check out the penthouse. Keep the change,' he said and walked out the bar.

Thomas picked up the note and watched John confidently walk out the bar. What did he know?

But there was something about what he said ...

No. He fished his mobile out of his pocket, he had to make a call.

Back in his office Pablo hung the phone up.

Maybe. This was a chance, and he had to take it. So Smith had given Ron a hiding but he was fat and old. Pablo was smarter. Now he knew where Smith was heading.

He called Skinny.

'Skinny, get hold of Biscuits, and right now. I need you and him at the hotel in fifteen. You wanted the job, you got it, but it needs patience. It's a waiting game, could be a long night.'

He hung up the phone and placed it on the desk, and then used the desk phone to call room service and ordered coffee.

As a prison this wasn't so bad he decided, at least it had a bathroom and he could get fed and watered. And it was safe and out the way.

With luck, and if he was careful by the time the sun came up everything would be resolved.

Chapter Seventeen

As he headed for the strip he checked his phone. No calls. It had now been nearly six hours since his conversation with Patrick. It looked like he would have to deal with this without getting any help. Not bothering to conceal himself anymore he caught the monorail back to the MGM Grand and then crossed over walking back down the strip, which despite the rain was as busy as ever. He skirted the Mandalay Bay and made for the golf course, and dug one of the Glock's out of the bag. He shoved it down the back of his trousers and concealed the bag inside the hedge again, then entered the hotel and went up to his room.

He got the binoculars and focused on the Penthouse. There was a dim light on in one part of it, but the rest was in darkness. There was no sign of any movement, but the blinds were still drawn. He sat very still for a long time, watching, waiting, hoping for a sign. He knew this was a 50-50 call. He could march straight in and start kicking in doors but there was every chance that if she was there she was sitting watching TV or eating dinner with Pablo, which would mean a pointless stand-off. Or, she could be buried out in the desert. Or she could be in a totally different city or state somewhere. He looked long and hard at the hotel down below. The place was open to him, Pablo had nobody left who could get in the way as far as he or George knew, so he just had to decide.

His phone rang, he didn't recognise the number but he answered anyway.

'John, it's Patrick.'

'Hey Patrick, anything in it?'

'John, where are you now?'

'In Vegas. Watching the Acropolis.'

'OK. Stay clear. This is rolling fast.'

'Does this mean you're going to get over here and have a look?'

'I'm in the Vegas field office right now. We just seized three serving FBI agents, and now we're on our way to arrest two of Las Vegas PD's finest, one of them a lieutenant.'

'Jesus. I said I wanted it looked at quick, but I never expected you to get it moving like this.'

'Like I said John, it's rolling fast. Coincidentally, I am in charge of the department that investigates exactly this kind of crime. I believe we should be better than this John. The FBI are not perfect by any means, but there's a clear line and it's been crossed by a mile.'

'So what's next?'

'Well speaking bluntly, we're busy. Like I said we have got to swing by some police officer's houses. This Pablo Escola, he has been paying off cops, the justice department, the FBI, probably even the man from the IRS for years. It was right there as soon as I looked at it. I could have got my most junior guy, hell even the janitor to take a look and it would have been obvious. I knew in five minutes I had to act.'

'So what about Pablo?'

'We're picking him up after the cops. I got someone watching. We know he's somewhere in the hotel.'

'Have you got enough do you think?'

'Everyone is singing John, so far they can't stop talking. So yeah, it's looking good. I'm real glad you called.'

'OK, well I am too. I think I'm not too far from finishing my work here now. I think I know where Abby is.'

'Right, well I will be in touch. And John, stay well away from the Acropolis OK? Don't go anywhere near the place.'

'OK Patrick, talk to you soon.'

So the decision had been made for him. He'd have to apologise to Patrick later. John checked his watch, just gone 2am. He pushed the Glock into his waistband, picked up the passkey and left the hotel.

He jogged across the road and walked up the steps into the Acropolis. As usual, there were plenty of people around so he wasn't worried about Patrick's comment about watching the hotel, his was just another face in the crowd.

He entered the building and crossed Reception heading for the door he had been through on his last visit, which was now standing wide open. He walked through into the large office behind, there were a couple of people working but they took no notice of him. The door on the other side was also open, and he saw a cleaner with a vacuum cleaner working in the corridor beyond. He followed it round to the glass panel door which was also propped open and headed for the lift. All the doors in the corridor here were closed and everywhere was silent as he passed by. If Abby was just sitting in the penthouse he was going to end up looking pretty stupid, Richard would no doubt ask why he hadn't checked there first. But he always trusted his instincts, they had definitely kept him alive. As when he had been here previously the lift doors in front of him were standing open so he walked in and pressed the 'P' button. The doors slid closed and the lift climbed away up to the top of the hotel.

Once at the roof level the doors opened again. John pushed himself into the corner of the lift and took the Glock out. The penthouse was silent. The top half of the back wall of the lift was a mirror, which meant he could use it to see out. This was useful but it also meant anyone waiting outside would be able to see him too.

Nothing he could do about it, so he got on with it.

There was a simple square lobby which was lit by lamps on the wall. To the right he could see an opening to a room but from where he was standing there was nothing else he could make out. He ducked well down low and cautiously looked out round the doors. The lobby was empty, and from his viewpoint the opening to the right led to a large darkened room with all the blinds pulled. John calculated the far wall was the one visible from his hotel. Carefully he leaned out further and looked to his left. There was a closed wooden door, and a small table, and nothing else. He wedged the table to stop the lift doors closing again and made his way over to the opening, hugging the wall by the lift as he went. Once at the corner he peered round into the room, which was big, very untidy and smelt stale as if there was no air. In front of him was a long u-shaped sofa arrangement, with a low glass table in the middle. The only light was in from the lobby or the neon from the strip through the blinds. He crossed over to the far side and looked in again. Now he could see all the way into the room. There was a large round dining table ringed with chairs at the far end. There was no sign of life, the place was silent as a grave. He entered the room and slowly made his way around, treading carefully in the gloom. He took in the large screen TV, white powder on the table and dirty dishes everywhere. He circled the dining area and turned right through another opening which led into a long state of the art kitchen which had the blind open at one window and was lit by the glow from outside. The room didn't look like it had ever been used. It ended with a huge fridge freezer and a door on the right. He stood to the side and slowly opened the door. Behind was much darker, and it appeared to be a simple corridor with closed doors on the left. John guessed that it had to lead back to the lobby at the top. It was completely empty, and there was no sound from anywhere. He slowly and silently made his way down and opened the first door. This was obviously the master bedroom, which was a mess, there was a large unmade bed and clothes scattered around the floor. At the far end on the right was an en-suite bathroom. Both rooms were completely empty. Leaving the door open he moved along the corridor and opened the next. This was a bathroom, apart from some towels thrown on the floor there was nothing to see here either. The next room was the first one which interested him. It was a much smaller bedroom, and it was also a mess.

John checked the corridor again and closed the door. He turned on the lamp standing on the bedside cabinet and then stood in the middle of the room trying to make sense of it. There was a double bed against the far wall with the covers everywhere, he looked at it more closely and saw there was blood among the other stains present. He reached into his back pocket, put on the gloves and looked at the bedside table and the floor around the bed. There were squares of blackened foil and syringes lying around and two empty vodka bottles. Next to the door was a bloody handprint and the plasterboard was damaged around the frame. John kicked around broken glasses with the toe of his boot and saw more stains on the carpet and then opened the door and stepped back into the corridor. With the light from the bedroom lamp glowing he could see more clearly now. Ahead of him there were two more doors, one on the left and one on the right. He walked up to the end and tried the right door; as he had expected it was the one that opened to the lobby he had seen earlier. He left that door open and then turned and went back to the last door, which was standing not fully closed. He could see it was full dark in the room through the narrow gap. He prodded it further open with the Glock. With the light from the bedroom lamp and the lobby he could see that the room was in the middle of some construction, the walls were unfinished and it had a bare concrete floor. It looked roughly square and didn't appear to have any windows. He was tempted to ignore it, but he still hadn't found Abby and realised he needed to check it properly just in case so stepped down into the room, pushing the door fully open as he did so.

He took two steps across the floor and then felt the cold muzzle of a gun pressed firmly against the base of his skull. He froze, and the Glock was yanked from his hand, and then he felt like a truck had slammed into him. He was sent flying into the middle of the room, landing on his knees and falling onto his front. Trying to work out what had happened and instinctively defending himself he rolled over twice and then jumped to his feet facing the door. A bright light was suddenly snapped on and he blinked forcing his eyes into focus. Skinny was standing watching with a big grin on his face.

'Not so tough now smart guy,' he said slowly.

Now all the open doors downstairs made sense. He had walked straight into it. Idiot. He only had himself to blame; he had only been thinking of finding Abby. As a result he'd ignored all the warning signs, and there had been plenty of them.

He wondered how they had known he would be coming.

'Thomas,' he said aloud as the realisation dawned on him.

Skinny applauded sarcastically.

'Right on! No loyalty to his Brit brother! That asshole was grassing on you the second you left the bar. And now you're all mine to deal with. And I'm really going to enjoy this.'

Apart from the gun in his hand John wasn't too worried about Skinny, but the other man in the room standing next to him was much more of a concern.

He was a giant, a freak of nature. Easily the biggest man John had ever seen, and not just his height which John calculated was even taller than Robert. He was wide too, and his thighs were bigger than John's waist. He was wearing what appeared to be dungarees and a red shirt. John watched him warily; the man had sparse black hair under a filthy baseball cap and sunken piggy eyes. He had a ghostly complexion and was sweating and twitching, never still. Standing there his huge hands were at the same height as his knees. His fingers were studded with chunky rings that looked like wheel nuts.

So this is what had happened, this man had just pushed him. It was literally as if he had been run over. John stared at him stunned. Skinny did the introductions.

'Oh yeah! You like this guy right? Mr Smith, this is Biscuits. Biscuits, meet Mr Smith. He's kind of a pain in the ass.'

Biscuits took a step forward and without realising he was doing it John took one back.

Skinny moved and slammed the door shut, and then locked it putting the key in his jacket pocket. He looked at John triumphantly.

'Hey John, can I call you John?'

'Fine,' John replied without taking his eyes off Biscuits and moving slowly to his right, attempting to stay in the centre of the room.

'Well John, there's good news and there's bad news. What do you want first pal?'

'I think I'll take the good please Skinny.'

'We ain't gonna kill ya. Pablo wants to send you home so's everyone can see what he did.'

'Right. Very magnanimous of him, and the bad?'

'Biscuits is really gonna hurt you. And I ain't a bit sorry.'

John had to agree that was on the cards. He quickly took in his surroundings; the room was not that big and he could easily get trapped in a corner in which case it would be all over in seconds, Biscuits would pummel the life out of him. All he could do was try and keep out of the man's immense reach. Skinny was hovering excitedly a few feet in front of the door holding the gun, behind him to one side there was a stack of cement bags and some lengths of timber and on the other side the light came from a builder's lamp on a stand. It looked like the room was being fitted out as a sauna or maybe a gym.

Biscuits had a weird expression on his face like he was trying to smile. It was impossible to tell if he even knew where he was, his eyes were like black pinpricks in the massive face. He took two lumbering steps forward and began swinging his huge arms, John danced back but still felt the wind.

He was in real trouble here, and he had to try and think clearly. Normally John was good in a fight because he could always keep calm, and forever had a surprise up his sleeve. But that was no good in this situation; he could never get close enough to Biscuits to do him any real damage without being totally exposed. Even if he was able to time it right and get in between the mighty swings and land a punch he still wouldn't be able to get free again safely. And he doubted one single blow would have that much effect, but there would be no time for a second. John kept himself very fit, and if it came down to it then he knew he would be able to outlast this freak but that meant doing it without getting hit, which was impossible. One good punch from one of those hands and it would be game over, it would only end one way and that meant badly for John.

He glanced at Skinny who was chuckling and waving the gun around. There had to be a way, had to be. He kept moving, circling from one side to the other, thinking hard, then it came to him. There was something he could do, at least try anyway. Without taking his eyes off Biscuits his brain went into overdrive as he worked out how he could maybe turn this around, but it was going to be difficult. It was a long shot, but all he could think of. Go for it. No choice. No choice at all. He decided to take a dummy run first.

He took a deep breath and stood up to his full height, which was not much at all compared to Biscuits, and with exaggerated steps feinted right and then immediately darted to his left and ducked down. Biscuits moved to his left as expected and then when John moved he lurched and immediately swung his right; narrowly missing John who jumped back up again ending up in the same place he had started from.

So it was maybe possible, but difficult. Biscuits was uncoordinated in his movements, almost like a toddler. John started edging round to his right, keeping his distance and getting nervous of the wall which was now not far behind him. Biscuits turned with him and began to close in. John moved left and then ran straight at Biscuits keeping to his right and ducking down.

With a growl and a grunt Biscuits swung his left fist, which John ducked but Biscuits was twisting and he managed to grab John's jacket and threw him back in a heap on the floor.

Skinny let out a loud cheer.

John got to his feet and moved back. He was getting dangerously close to the corner. He had only one shot left at this. He repeated the same movement, but this time rotating to his right, trying to line up but at the same time doing everything he could to distance himself from the corner, which was becoming increasingly difficult. This was it, all or nothing. He drew Biscuits in until it was nearly too late, then ran to his left, again ducking down, missing the huge right that was thrown. But again Biscuits recovered and twisted around, then lunged out with his left which caught John a glancing blow across his right eye. Glancing, but still enough to send John sliding over the floor on his front.

He ended up against the wall on his side, stunned and shaken and weakly trying to stand.

Skinny began whooping and hollering.

'Woo-hoo! You finish that motherfucker Biscuits, pound him bad. Break every fucking bone!'

As quick as he could John crawled away, trying to distance himself from Biscuits who he knew would be coming in for the kill, he was hurting badly and trying to clear his head. He could feel warm blood running down his face and neck. But his plan had partially worked, he was in pain, but he realised he was very close to where he wanted to be. Without looking up properly he calculated where Skinny was and with a groan dropped his head. He didn't know how much time he had before Biscuits was on him but it could only be seconds. He groaned again and Skinny's feet appeared in front of him as he egged Biscuits on.

With a shake of his head John sprang to his feet right on top of Skinny who startled, fell back and John grabbed his gun arm at the wrist, pulled it up and began twisting. The gun went off twice, bullets sailing harmlessly over John's shoulder. Using both hands John carried on twisting all the time pushing Skinny backwards. The gun fell and clattered to the floor. With a wrench John broke Skinny's arm and then punched him twice hard in the face and then whirled around watching Biscuits while readying himself to go for the gun.

Biscuits was standing stock still about ten feet away with a surprised look on his face, a crimson flower shaped stain slowly getting bigger on his chest. He sank to his knees with a grunt, and then collapsed on the floor.

John turned back to Skinny and stamped hard on the hand on his good arm twice. Skinny shrieked and tried to roll into a ball, but John pulled him onto his back and searched him, retrieving the Glock, a mobile phone and the door key. He unlocked, picked up Skinny's gun and threw it out the door, then walked over to Biscuits, and rolled him over.

He had been shot in the chest, a sucking wound. He was still alive, his unfocussed eyes moving slowly from side to side and breathing shallowly, mouth open. There wasn't much John could do so he called 911 and requested an ambulance urgently and then dragged Skinny over. He pulled off the other man's jacket making him yell out in pain and then balled it up and pressed it onto Biscuits' chest. Then he got Skinny's forearm on the good arm but with the ruined hand and pushed it down hard onto the jacket.

'Right Skinny, you shot your buddy Biscuits. You have to keep the pressure on. If you let up even slightly I'm just gonna shoot you. That clear?'

Skinny nodded frantically and leaned down on Biscuits sobbing loudly.

John went down on one knee.

'Skinny, where's Abby?'

Skinny looked up at him.

'Look, Pablo said, he told us ....'

'Fuck Pablo. Fuck him. He's next believe me. Where is she?'

'Outside. She's by the pool. But you're too late,' Skinny whispered dropping his head.

John stood up and left the room, collecting Skinny's gun on the way. He turned right and walked down the corridor and through the kitchen into the dining area. On his right were floor to ceiling folding glass doors, with the blinds pulled. He yanked the nearest one open and stepped out. He was on a large oval patio with a swimming pool in the middle. There were loungers dotted around, and lying on the ground between two was Abby.

John ran over, it looked like Skinny had been right; he was too late. Abby was lying half on her side. She was wearing nothing but an open dressing gown. John knelt down next to her and checked for her pulse. It was there, but rapid and weak. He checked her for any injuries; she was completely covered in bruises and had dried blood over her legs. He had no idea what to do, so he wrapped her up in the dressing gown and lifted her up and made for the lift.

He kicked the table out from between the doors and bent down hitting the 'G' button with his fingertips. The doors closed and the lift descended, John willing it to go faster. He caught sight of himself in the mirror, his face was a mess. His right eye was nearly closed and his face and collar were caked in blood. He remembered the rings on Biscuits' fingers.

Chapter Eighteen

John watched the floor numbers slowly changing downward and looked closely at Abby. Her lips were blue and she was white as a sheet. Her eyes suddenly flicked open and she looked at him confused, but then she was out again. The doors opened and moving as quickly as possible John moved back through the bowels of the hotel bursting out into Reception. Still nobody stopped him but people moved out of his way as he made it to the doors and went outside. He could hear a siren getting louder so he ran down the steps and met the ambulance as it pulled up. As they climbed out the paramedics spotted him and ran over.

'I don't know what has happened, I know she's taken something, but I don't have any idea what,' John said.

One of the paramedics ran back to the ambulance and unloaded a stretcher, the legs folding down. John moved over and laid her on it and immediately the paramedics got to work, checking her over and giving her oxygen and fixing a drip. John hovered around, increasingly anxious. The paramedics finished doing they could right there on the ground and hurriedly put Abby into the ambulance, obvious concern written all over them.

John followed them over to the open doors and peered in. One of the paramedics looked up and came over.

'So you don't have any idea on what she's taken, what she's on?' he asked.

'No, sorry, I never met her before. But there are syringes and all sorts of other crap in the bedroom, you know, signs that she has been using something.'

'So you don't know what's happened to her?'

'No idea. I just found her like that. Will she be OK?'

'I can't tell you that. We need to get her to the emergency room.'

'You must have some idea, what are her chances?'

The paramedic sighed.

'Really, I can't say. But she's got a fight on her hands. I'd say another hour before you got to her it would be all over.'

John felt a coldness sinking through him.

'Where are you taking her?'

'Mercy, it's closest.'

'There's another man upstairs, he's been shot. I called that in before I found her.'

The paramedic frowned.

'OK, well we'll get on the radio.'

He leaned closer and turned John's head.

'You should come with us, you need to get that looked at.'

John pulled away.

'No. I got something I need to do first.'

The paramedic shrugged and pulled the doors shut, and then the ambulance was off with tyres screeching and siren blaring.

John turned and looked up at the hotel.

'Right. This ends now.'

In his office Pablo stared down at the phone on his desk in front of him. He centred it and made it even to the edges.

There had been no contact, but Pablo couldn't ring Skinny in case John Smith was just entering the penthouse.

'Patience,' he said aloud.

Around him was just silence, even the normal hotel sounds were more muted than usual.

He poured himself another cup of coffee and waited.

Like a robot John walked up the steps and through the doors; then marched across Reception and entered the back of house area again, he hoped for the last time. He crossed the big office and went into the corridor beyond. As he made his way down he crossed from side to side opening every door, flinging them open wide. Most of the rooms were empty at that hour, but the two or three that had people in them looked at him in surprise. He carried on going and then went past the glass door. The corridor with no names on any of the doors. The lift stood open at the end.

He repeated the same process in this corridor, but moving more cautiously now and trying the handles gently. The last thing he needed was if someone opened fire from inside, the bullets would come through these doors like they were paper. He went through them in turn and then came to the final door on his left and just suddenly got a feeling. Carefully he tried the handle.

Locked.

Then he heard the sound of a toilet being flushed inside.

He knew. This was it. It was time.

He lined himself up, and stepped back. Then he raised his right leg and drew it back and then kicked out forward. The sole of his boot connected with the handle, the frame splintered and the door crashed open. Immediately John followed through and burst into the room. Pablo Escola was in the process of sitting down in the chair with a look of shock on his face, which turned to terror when John launched himself across the desk and then dragged Pablo back across the top of it by his shirt.

John threw him to the floor and Pablo cowered against the wall. John pulled him up and punched him twice in the face, a left then a right and then slammed him against the wall so hard the plasterboard disintegrated behind him. Then he hurled him out into the corridor and as Pablo tried desperately to crawl away began kicking him hard around his backside and ribs. Tiring of that he picked Pablo up and began throwing him from one side to another, interspersing it with punches.

In truth, John was enjoying himself. Pablo had a lot to answer for.

Eventually Pablo curled up into a ball on the floor and stared up with his arms raised.

'Stop! Stop, please stop,' he cried.

John stood next to him and looked down. Pablo's nose was bleeding heavily, probably broken. His lips were swollen and bloody and his left eye was starting to close. His shirt was torn and dirty.

He was broken.

John hauled him to his feet.

'Let's go Pablo.'

He forced Pablo's head under his arm and dragged him off down the corridor. It was slow going; Pablo frequently tripped or tried to stand and John just got his neck in a tighter hold and swung him around as he pulled. He walked into the main office and the few people in there stared as they passed, but nobody made any attempt to intervene. He entered Reception with the same result. As he neared the main doors a pair of Paramedics walked in.

John stopped them and pointed to the way he had come, still holding Pablo in a headlock.

'Go through that office and follow the corridor, there's a lift at the end. You want the penthouse; when you're up there go through the door on the left then the first on the right. Gunshot wound to the chest. He is a big fella, I mean really big. You'll want the stretcher, but be quick, he's in bad way,' he told the bemused paramedics, and then continued walking out of the hotel.

He reached the top of the steps and then threw Pablo down, as hard as he could, and followed him. As he reached the bottom a police car pulled up, followed by another, with a dark blue sedan at the rear. The whole area was lit by a bright array of red and blue flashing neon. Cops jumped out and ran over and one stopped John as he bent down to grab Paulo.

'Step away sir. Put your hands on your head and step away.'

John looked at him and shook his head.

'No, I'm not done here yet.'

The cop grabbed John by the arm.

'This is not a request boy. I don't need any encouragement to take you downtown after the night I been having.'

John went nose to nose with the cop.

'Did you call me boy? I must be what, fifteen years older than you?'

'OK, let's all calm down.'

John turned and saw Patrick climbing out of the lead sedan and walking over, holding his FBI badge out high.

The cop pushed John away and stood glowering, his hand hovering near his revolver.

Ignoring him Patrick pulled Pablo to his feet and looked at John.

'Good to see you again John. I thought I told you to stay well away? It looks like you been busy, and it looks like Mr Escola must have fallen down those steps judging by his injuries.'

John relaxed.

'Nice to see you too Patrick. So what's the score? '

'We're a lot of points up John. We've collared the cops, including one I believe you know.'

John looked closely at the cars and saw Frank MacMillan in the back of one. Suddenly he felt very tired; it had been a long night.

He handed Patrick Skinny's gun, still wearing gloves.

'There was a shooting earlier, paramedics are up in the penthouse now dealing with it. The guy that did it also fell down some stairs, he's up there too. This is the gun.'

Patrick held the gun between his thumb and forefinger right at the edge of the butt and yelled at an agent to get an evidence bag.

'Jesus John, do you ever take a break?'

'Patrick, I need to get to Mercy hospital. I found Abby up in the penthouse; she's in a bad way.'

'OK, I'll drive you myself. Just let me get things moving here.'

'Thanks Patrick.'

John watched as Pablo was bundled into the back of one of the cop cars, and Patrick organised the FBI agents who disappeared into the hotel.

Patrick gestured over to John to join him and they climbed into one of the sedans and set off for the hospital.

On the way Patrick filled John in on the night's work.

'Well, we've got a list of evidence longer than your arm. We found witness statements, evidence, blood tests everything, all pointing to Pablo. It was all hidden but they kept it all, the FBI out here, the cops; they didn't get rid of anything. My guess is in case he suddenly didn't want to pay, but a lot of people are gonna go down for this. They are already pointing fingers at each other and naming names. It unfolded just like that, everybody suddenly very keen to talk to us. And if you hadn't picked up the phone then it would have carried on, at least until somebody wised up and popped Pablo, which by the sounds of it was getting more and more likely.'

'So Pablo isn't going to walk away?'

'Not this time. No way, I got about a dozen FBI and PD people up to their necks in this. The charge sheets are being drawn up. I mean we've got all we need, but to cap it all we discovered a witness, a young girl who survived. I got an agent driving into Arizona right now. This poor girl was raped and beaten by Pablo and left for dead but she survived. A woman found her and called 911. It was hushed up by the FBI, and the PD, and swept under the carpet. Her parents managed to get her away, but we located her and she is going to talk. We got all we need already anyway, but this is going to bury Pablo, no question at all.'

'What about his father?'

'I can't comment on that right now because I don't know, but I promise you I got people looking into it.'

'OK.'

'You know, the cops been busy tonight. Witnesses saw some guy beat the crap out of the manager of this strip bar called Honeys. Just happens that Pablo Escola owns it. I can't imagine you would know anything about it.'

John smiled.

'Nothing at all Patrick.'

They reached the hospital and John got out, promising to call Patrick in the morning. He walked in and asked at the

Reception counter and was directed to the emergency room. He made his way through the maze of corridors and then asked again at the desk there. He was told to wait so he sat down. Half an hour later a harried looking doctor came out. She guided John over to a viewing window and he could see Abby about halfway down, with tubes and wires all over her.

'She has no ID, do you know her name?' the doctor asked.

'Yeah, her name is Abby Cromwell, she's British.'

'Can I ask your connection to her?'

'None. It's a long story. I came out here to find her, her father is worried about her. Tonight I tracked her down to the Acropolis hotel. I found her lying down totally out of it by the pool. I called for an ambulance and that's it, I never met her before or even spoken to her.'

'We have notified the police. They will want to talk to you. She's been raped, more than once.'

'Yeah I guessed that. There was a lot of blood on her. I know who did it. The FBI have already got him.'

'Right, well …'

'Is she going to be alright?'

The doctor looked at him wearily, then raised her eyes up to the ceiling and sighed.

'It's very early. She's had a massive overdose. Heroin we believe, but we are not one hundred percent on what she has taken, it could even be some kind of cocktail. She has a large amount of injuries, but none serious. There's no set pattern in dealing with this, it all depends on exactly what she took and how much, and unfortunately, we have no idea. But we're doing everything we can.'

'OK, thank you very much. I'll phone her dad and let him know and I'll come back tomorrow.'

He turned and started to walk back the way he had come.

'Wait.'

The doctor took hold of his arm, looked up at his head and half smiled, checked her watch, then pointed to a small room to the side.

'Come and sit in here. That needs sutures. Sometimes even heroes need a helping hand.'

John looked at her reluctantly and went to walk away, but she held on tight to his arm.

'Seriously, come on. It needs treating. You'll bleed everywhere, I can see to it nice and easy right now. If you go through to the ER you'll have to wait.'

John gave in, and followed the doctor across, then sat still and quiet while the doctor fixed up his head. She asked him a few questions about Abby, but he genuinely couldn't answer them, other than why he was in the city in the first place and how he had come to find her.

John thanked the doctor, left the hospital and called Richard, explaining very carefully about Abby, breaking the news as gently as possible. Richard told him he'd be on the first plane out. John hung up and looked for a taxi then made his way back to the Mandalay Bay.

Chapter Nineteen

After a late breakfast John wandered over to the Acropolis hotel. Everything looked pretty much the same as yesterday, but he spotted George talking with a short red-haired man and a second big Slavic looking man with a shaved head on the steps. He was in two minds whether to join them but George noticed him and with a wide smile came over.

He shook John's hand vigorously.

'I'm still real sketchy on everything that went down, but Pablo won't be back, that's for sure. I can't get any real information from the cops, but he's definitely out of the picture. And I know I got you to thank for that.'

'All I did was get Abby. As far as I know Pablo realised the game was up, ran for it and fell down these highly dangerous steps after colliding with a wall or two inside,' John replied.

George smiled even wider and led John away from the red-haired man who was looking at them curiously.

'New York are happy enough, although that probably ain't the right word. There's still a big pot of money missing, but that ain't got shit to do with me and you. They are sending some guys over to get the Acropolis back on its feet, until then I may as well get my five cents worth. That's Shaun Farley there with the red hair, he's got his work cut out now. The other guy is Stefan, who was Pablo's right hand. But he's a good man, worked for Francesco a long time, sometimes in this business you got to deal with people that normally you'd cross the street to avoid, and Stefan is good at that. Francesco asked him to take care of Pablo, and I'd say he's been doing it and doing it well considering. He's kept him alive, which is a near miracle. And he's been able to keep him from drowning in all the shit he's got himself into. Technically, he's out of work, but I know a lot of people who will give him a job, no question. He was my man on the inside John, playing both sides at the same time I guess but for the right reasons. I got a million other questions for you John, but I got a feeling you don't wanna listen to them or answer any.'

He held out his hand and John shook it.

'I kind of feel like it got out of control if I'm honest George, I didn't expect any of this. I suppose I thought that I could maybe have a problem with Pablo persuading Abby to at least call her dad but this is something else altogether. Still, in the end, I did what I came here for.'

George nodded and looked at John's head.

'Nasty, who did that?'

'I walked into a door.'

'Yeah, you got to watch those things. Listen, tonight dinner is on me. It's about time you enjoyed being in Las Vegas in my opinion.'

'George, I came out here to find Abby. I found her, but I don't know if I was in time. She's in intensive care at the hospital. It's not looking good, so I'm not feeling like celebrating.'

'I get that. But thank you anyway, and let me know. The invitation is wide open.'

John nodded.

'Thanks George. FBI still around?'

'Not really. They been searching but mostly around Pablo's office and in the finance offices, I think they've got a couple of guys still up in the penthouse. But they don't seem interested in anything else; they haven't asked any awkward questions as far I know.'

John's phone rang; he excused himself and answered. It was Patrick, anxious to meet up. More and more evidence had been uncovered; he was a very happy man. They arranged to get together at the South Precinct later.

John looked at his watch, and made another call. Then promising George he would be back later he headed to the Mandalay Bay. He walked around toward the golf course and retrieved the bag, and took out his ID's and the wig and threw in the Glock. He wandered around the rear of the hotel and threw the bag with the guns and the gloves into a big waste bin, then went back up to his room and packed. Half an hour later he was in a taxi on the way to airport, and three hours after that on a plane back to London.

Four weeks later he returned to Richard Cromwell's house. This time he parked right outside. He picked up a box from the boot and walked up and rang the doorbell, which was answered by the smart Chinese lady again. If she recognised him she didn't show it, and politely asked him to wait in the hallway.

John stood at the bottom of the stairs, but the door to the office opened almost immediately and Richard appeared. He walked quickly over and embraced John, who stood stiffly unsure what to do.

'Thank you. I don't have the words. Thank you for what you have done.'

'Is Abby OK?' John asked surprised. He had been delaying coming to see Richard, putting it off as long as possible.

'She is home now; and the good news is she's getting better every day. I've been trying to call you but your phone doesn't work.'

There was a good reason for that. John had destroyed the SIM card before he flew home, something he always did at the end of every job. He shrugged apologetically. Richard asked the Chinese lady for some coffee.

'That is great news. I'm really glad she's well. I've got something for you,' John told him.

'I have something for you, too. Let's go into the office.'

Once they were inside and Richard was seated at his desk John placed the box on the table.

'What's this?' Richard asked him, looking at it with interest.

'One point five million dollars. Roughly a million pounds, give or take.'

Richard stared up at him perplexed, and then opened the box which was stuffed with hundred-dollar bills.

He picked a bundle up and looked at it wonderingly.

'You are an amazing man John Smith. I never expected this. You should keep it, you earned every penny. Or cent as it were.'

'No, it's yours. It was stolen from you after all. It turned out the rightful owners didn't want it.'

Richard shook his head with a smile and then passed a thick envelope over to John.

'This is your balance payment, with a bonus.'

John nodded his thanks and took the envelope and put it in his jacket pocket. He didn't need to count it. The Chinese lady appeared with the coffee and poured it into two cups. John took a sip, and steeled himself to ask the question he was dreading.

'So, what's the story with Abby? Will she ever be, you know, this sounds terrible I know, but back to normal?'

Richard ran both hands over his face and paused before replying.

'I appreciate you asking, and it's actually not bad news. Not all bad, anyway. I've got the best doctors on it, but it's a long road. HIV tests, detox, rehab, you name it. Months of not knowing. But she's talking and she is brighter. She spends half her time here, and half in the clinic, but she is definitely improving and she seems a lot happier now. She can walk and talk, I'm quietly optimistic.'

'Has she said anything?'

'Not really, other than she blames herself.'

'Has she told you what happened?'

'Well, bits and pieces. She says she got out of depth very quickly. At first it was fun, Pablo basically was showing her off. But then there were some arguments, mostly about money. Pablo was insisting that she got more out of me, but Abby refused, that wasn't why she was there. She realised too late that he was bad news and was going to stay in Caesars, but Pablo found out all about it and came up with this idea of basically locking her away, he started giving her some drugs to keep her quiet when she protested. It seems like he got her hooked, but I don't really know. I have no idea about that world. But it was very close. You saved her life John, no question about that at all. The doctors have all confirmed it.'

John shook his head.

'It was my mistake Richard. I should have just barged into the penthouse in the first place, but because it was always in darkness I ruled it out. Nobody ever seemed to be there.'

'I don't think you can blame yourself. You knew nothing about any of this a week ago, and from what the police have told me there was a whole lot of trouble totally unconnected with Abby.'

John nodded and the two men stood in silence for a while. John looked at his watch.

'By the way I heard Francesco was released last week,' Richard told him. 'I'm hoping he'll contact me. I understand that he has you to thank. It seems you did the best for everyone, well done.'

'Nothing I did I promise you. It turns out Pablo was not a popular man, all I did was push a few buttons and let the rest take its natural course.'

'Well, I owe you a huge debt, Please, stay for lunch, I would love to hear more about it.'

John smiled, but shook his head.

'Richard I'm sorry but I have to go. By the way, is Charles around?'

'Charles? I think so, let me get him.'

'Thanks. Don't tell him it's me OK?'

Richard looked surprised but got up and went from the room. John followed him and then walked out the front door, leaving it open behind him. After Vegas, London seemed colder than ever and despite the short stay and then all the weeks he had been back it felt like he was still getting used to it. He walked out onto the steps and waited.

He heard footsteps behind him and turned.

Charles was walking down nonchalantly and realised too late it was John. Startled, he turned to run but John was quicker and tripped him. Charles fell down the remaining steps, hit the ground hard and cried out, then sat looking up at John.

Richard appeared on top of the steps closely followed by Bruno, who looked concerned, and started to make his way down.

John held his hand up.

'Hang on there Richard will you please. This will only take a second.'

He walked down the steps then squatted next to Charles and spoke quietly.

'Why did you tip off Pablo Charles? I can't work it out at all. It can't have been for money. He hasn't got any and you've got more than you'll ever need.'

Charles stared at him fearfully.

'I didn't! I swear! It must have been James …'

John put his finger on Charles' lips.

'Ssssh. Don't lie to me. The problem you've got now is you really didn't need me as an enemy. I mean you really didn't.'

'But …'

'Charles you're gonna be spending the rest of your life looking over your shoulder. Every single day.'

Charles stared at him, beginning to comprehend.

John's mobile phone rung suddenly shattering the silence, He glanced at the screen and answered.

'Hello?'

'Is that Simon? I have a message for you.'

'Great. I'll call you back.'

John hung up and then stood, and pulled Charles to his feet. Then, with a wave to Richard he walked calmly down the drive, got into his car and drove away, without looking back.

CPSIA information can be obtained
at www.ICGtesting.com
Printed in the USA
BVHW031109140619
551042BV00002B/233/P